# a yorkshire carol

## JENNIE GOUTET

*Dedicated to Rod Stormes—you're a Bobby Dazzler and it'd never 'av 'appened wi'out yer.*

# CHAPTER 1

## LONDON, NOVEMBER 22, 1815

"Oohoo!" Mrs. Issot cried, waving a letter for her daughter as she entered the canary-colored drawing room of their modest London house. Juliana sat on a cushioned settee and absently coaxed a knot out of her terrier's brown fur while enjoying a rare and delicious moment with a novel. As much as she thrived on the London social scene, Juliana's peace of mind could only be restored by solitude.

"Your godmother has written, inviting you to spend Christmas in Yorkshire since she cannot be in London this year. And this time, I really think you must accept her invitation."

Resigned to the loss of her peace, Juliana closed the small, leather-bound book and set it on the side table as her dog lifted an ear and peered at the interloper.

"Do you, Mother?" She knew her tone was not encouraging, but that could not be helped. She loved her godmother but preferred to keep their visits to London, where there was at least some novelty to be had.

"I do. Three times she has invited you to accompany her to Yorkshire before the start of the Season, and three times you have denied her. If you don't accept Mrs. Savile's invitation, she shall wash her hands of you at last. Besides, you must agree there is nothing like a Yorkshire Christmas."

Mrs. Issot, a plump and less vibrant version of her red-haired daughter, sat across from Juliana and felt the teapot on the table in front of her. Its contents were cold, and she leaned back in her chair.

"I should not like to offend my godmother, but perhaps that cannot be helped," Juliana replied, piqued at being forced to the point. "If she is only pleased with me on the condition that I travel to Yorkshire in the bitter cold, one might wonder if such conditional approbation is worth securing."

"Juliana, you know you are unjust." Frown lines appeared on Mrs. Issot's face, and Juliana knew that her mother's sense of obligation toward their wealthy Yorkshire neighbour—who had agreed to act as Juliana's godmother twenty-two years ago—made her anxious to show every consideration. "Mrs. Savile has bestowed her attention upon you most graciously...has been a kind and generous godmother. If all you do in return is to present her with an embroidered handkerchief each Christmas—"

"I detest embroidery and consider the act of doing it a precious-enough gift." Juliana raised her eyes and gave her mother a droll look.

"Please, my love. Do stop funning. I know you don't mean half the things you say, but others might be put off by behavior they consider to be too coming."

Juliana meant very well the things she said but did not insist. Her mother was made of different stuff, and where Juliana declared and decided, her mother placated and soothed, coaxed and coddled.

"Very well, Mother. But you must own that for all your professed love of Yorkshire, you have not been there to enjoy it these three Christmases past."

Mrs. Issot looked daunted for a moment before rallying.

"Well, it can hardly be reasonable for someone of my age to travel so far in the winter, but such a thing can hardly concern you. When you insist on walking Hazel or taking your Arabian out in all kinds of inclement weather?" Her mother brightened. "Why, that's another thing. You may accompany Willelm Armitage on Lord Darlington's fox hunt—or perhaps he will host his own this year."

Juliana allowed her gaze to settle across the room as the memory of the last fox hunt over Yorkshire territory came to mind. On that hunt, her jump over a stone wall had left Willelm yelling at her for her foolhardiness, then boasting afterwards of her skill when he thought she was not in hearing. The prospect did sound appealing. She had not participated in a single hunt since she'd left for London—not even to follow it with the other ladies in a carriage. Twice she had been invited to house parties for Christmas, but riding to the hounds had not been on the list of amusements.

Her mother, not wise enough to let this argument advance her work, continued. "I never did understand why you and Willelm did not make a match of it. You've had three Seasons, my love, and have not found someone to suit you, so why not him? You are already friends, so you need not fear he would be a disagreeable husband. And Mrs. Savile has assured me he will help make up the party. Perhaps..." She let the word dangle.

"My godmother must have windmills in her head if *that* is her purpose in—" Juliana stopped at the shocked look on her mother's face. "I am sorry, Mother. You need not scold me, for I know it was wrong of me to say so—but she *cannot* think we will suit. Why, Will and I have been friends since I was in leading strings, and not once did the idea of matrimony *to each other* cross our minds."

"Well, it is a shame that it does not, for I believe you would suit very well besides his being ahead in the world. I should so like to see you married well." Mrs. Issot spun around on her chair to look behind her. "Shall I ring for more hot water? No, I suppose we will eat dinner soon enough. But I am feeling a draught."

Juliana scooted Hazel from the settee onto the floor and stood. "I will ring for hot water." Perhaps she could distract her mother from the unwelcome Yorkshire mission. She waited until the footman came, gave him instructions, then resumed her seat.

"No matter what happens with Willelm, I believe you must go to Yorkshire, as I have said. You have turned down three of her invitations, and with the flimsiest of excuses. Mrs. Savile will begin to think you do not care for her, and that would be downright *cruel* after everything she has done, for she may not be long for this world."

Juliana drew her brows together at this surprising pronouncement. Her godmother was of much too placid a nature to complain if her ailment were of no consequence; and as much as Juliana did not relish a visit to Yorkshire, she had no wish to see her godmother fall ill—or worse.

Mrs. Issot had begun skimming the letter, and she pointed to the scrawl in the middle of the page. "See. Here she says, 'I am not walking as well as I used to and might stay confined in my sitting room for days at a stretch. The world seems to grind to a halt at times, as if there is nothing further to inspire me to live in it.'"

"See if that does not convince you," her mother added, piercing Juliana with her gaze. "You have no set plans. Besides, I don't think you could wish to be backward in any attention where your godmother is concerned."

Juliana shook her head, sobered by the news. "Of course not."

She fell silent. She did not precisely have plans, although she had hoped to have been invited to her friend's estate for Christmas. Caroline Fulham had catalogued a list of amusements should her older brother, a desirable catch, decide to host a Christmas party. Mr. Fulham was everything a young woman could wish for—humorous, well-liked, fine to look upon... solvent. But no invitation had been forthcoming, and it was already mid-November. Juliana's alternative would be to play nursemaid to her sister Lisbeth's girls, who were charming creatures when taken in small doses.

That reminded her. Juliana was soon to have a third niece or nephew, and that must surely mean she would have to travel to Yorkshire alone.

"You will not go with me, though, will you? Not with Lisbeth's confinement so near." Juliana raised an eyebrow and shook her head, already reading the answer on her mother's face. "And not in such cold weather. Will Father?"

"Your father will not know how to manage the house at Hutton Conyers without me there. I'm afraid you will have to go with Betty."

Juliana sighed audibly, though it was ill-bred. The very last thing she wished to do was return to Yorkshire, which she had been avoiding ever since she had escaped to London for her first Season three years ago. There was nothing precisely wrong with Yorkshire; it simply wasn't very exciting. And she had become convinced from her first Season that a match to someone with a spacious London house, in a more fashionable location and with access to the finest social engagements, would suit her very well. She had no interest in spinsterhood, which threat was starting to become a reality for her. And her godmother's Christmas party would not likely contain any eligible men. However, if her godmother was truly unwell, and Juliana was not invited elsewhere, the visit must be made.

"Very well. I will write to her with my acceptance." Pronouncing the words felt like a death knell, but her mother only smiled.

"I am sure you are doing the right thing. You can hardly have forgotten the pudding and the pantos and games...We've never managed to capture all those delightful traditions when we celebrate Christmas in London. And you shall taste a truly delicious Yorkshire pie again!"

Her mother's excited chatter only plunged Juliana's mood further.

"Read the letter for yourself. She has invited you for St. Nicholas's Day, which will be upon us before you know it. I will tell your father to secure your stagecoach billet and have Betty begin packing your trunks."

"Stay and wait for your hot water, Mother. I shall speak with Betty, and you can tell Father over dinner if you have not anticipated my surrender and done so already. I will have to leave in a fortnight if I am to arrive for St. Nicholas's Day." Juliana little looked forward to the preparations, although the thought that at least her wardrobe was a thing to be envied gave her a little cheer.

The footman arrived with the hot water, and Juliana left her mother to settle in to drink her tea. She exited into the corridor, with Hazel in front of her, and walked up the stairs, allowing her hand to trail along the smooth mahogany banister. For the first time in many months, she thought of her old friend, Willelm Armitage. He was closer in age to Lisbeth, but for some reason, they had never exchanged more than bare civilities, whereas there had been a time when Juliana and he had been inseparable. She supposed it was because Lisbeth didn't like to ride, and she didn't like to laugh. Willelm loved both.

Juliana did not write to him, of course, as they had no connection by either blood or marriage. She thought that a silly rule, though. Surely a woman might write to a friend who was male as easily as she might write to a female. But protocol was a cruel gaoler, and there were a great many things an unmarried woman might not do.

She entered her bedroom and sat at the desk, allowing

herself the luxury of brooding over the projected voyage. Yorkshire again! The last time she had seen Willelm was when he had come for the Season two years ago. How ridiculous he had seemed in London, and how out of place. He was practically a farmer, for all that he was a gentleman and now the squire of Studley Roger. He had a thick build—"stodgy," she had privately described him when in a funning humor—but she supposed he was the kind of person one would wish to hug if one needed it.

However, he had not fit in London society. Fine enough when dressed for the evening, but he had none of the elegance or languor one admired in the London gentlemen and certainly none of the excitement. She had seen him stand up a few times during his Season, and he had stood up with *her* until she told him she had not come to London to dance with her playmates. Then he never asked her again—nor had he paid her another morning visit.

The quill was in need of trimming, and Juliana did so before taking out a piece of paper from her desk drawer. Before she could begin her letter of acceptance, Hazel ambled over and sat next to Juliana's chair, looking up at her. Juliana put down her quill and picked up her dog instead, settling Hazel on her lap and scratching her neck in just the place the dog loved most.

"Well, Hazel. It seems a long journey in the cold awaits us. What do you think about that? Do you have any wish to return to Yorkshire?" The terrier laid its head on its paws and closed its eyes, and Juliana caressed its ears. "*Hmm!* My sentiments exactly."

Sharow Hall, Friday 26th November, 1815

My dear Temperance,

The Christmas season is almost upon us, and I am hoping—or perhaps scheming is a better word—to have the pleasure of a visit from my goddaughter Juliana. It has been three years since she has set foot in Sharow.

My mind has been busy with ideas on this topic, as I have just this day received a letter from Margarette Fudge with some matchmaking scheme she has concocted with Amelie Goodson for Christmas. I must write to Amelie at once. Had you something in the post from her as well?

If not, I aim to precipitate her letter and propose our own friendly wager on the matter since we are not to meet this year and I will not earn your shillings in the standard way through a game of whist. You've always had a ready spirit for fun, and I know you will not deny me this pleasure, despite your not having put off your blacks. And you must own that your Mr. Bolingbroke would have heartily approved of my scheme, for it will give you cause to smile again.

Margarette thinks to bring about a match for her great-nephew, the baron. Do you remember him? Last we met, she spoke of Lord Brooks, who had managed to evade all matrimonial lures set out for him, despite his being both titled and pleasing to the eye. As it turns out, he is at last forced to the altar in order to fill his coffers. *She* has engaged to find him a wife who will fill both his coffers and his heart and is already crowing over the anticipated success of her venture. Such a project can only turn Margarette's mind in a happier direction, for winters are never easy in her widowed state. And this must be the very thing for you as well. It has been six months since you've had to bid farewell to your dear Mr. Bolingbroke, and there is nothing shocking in participating in some innocent fun with your old friends.

Amelie was not to be outdone by Margarette and has promised to bring about a splendid match for her grand-daughter Odette, which I understand might necessitate a stay in London for the Season. Well! I refuse to be left behind. Do you remember my goddaughter? Juliana Issot is a charming York-shire girl with masses of red curls who comes from a genteel family that resided in Hutton Conyers not far from me. Now her parents rent a modest lodging in London to avoid the York-shire winters and stay within call of their grandchildren.

Juliana has enough pride and beauty to snare a duke. I do not propose she marry a duke, however. I have in mind for her a Yorkshireman! Mr. Willelm Armitage is squire of Studley Roger and is quite eligible besides being a fine young man. Raynald thinks highly of him, and you know Raynald is a very good judge of character. He married me, after all!

In case you think to decline my wager thinking the match is all but won, let me assure you that they have known each other from the cradle; and although I'm certain no matrimonial thought ever crossed Juliana's mind, Willelm is woven with different fibers. I am equally certain he has been soft on her from even before she left the schoolroom. It is unfortunate that worthy young men do not always appear in the guise of heroes to young ladies. And as Willelm is of a serious turn of mind, besides being of only average height and not above average looks, he is no different. If there is one thing that might help his cause, it is that, despite being little given to frivolity, when something amuses him, his somber expression positively cracks open in a grin, and his eyes light up as well. He and Juliana were once friends, but I do not believe they danced above twice in London, nor did they have much conversation there.

I aim to have them both at my house party for Christmas, along with your great-nephew and -niece, Anthony and Clarissa

Weld, who have already accepted my invitation. Just think! When you told me of their circumstance and how a month in the country would be just the thing, I did not know then that I would be able to entertain them so royally. My party is to last a full month, from St. Nicholas Day to Twelfth Night. And if Juliana and Willelm do not come to an agreement under those conditions, I will own myself beat.

My first difficulty will be to get Juliana to agree to come, but I believe the letter I sent out earlier this week should serve the purpose. You know how clumsy I have always been. Well, nothing has changed. I slipped and twisted my foot on the edge of a sinkhole that was quite hidden by the tall grass, and, as it is in a part of the property I rarely venture to, I had quite forgotten it was there. Not much harm done, although the local physician says I am to stay off my foot. But I may have exaggerated its severity with the goal of winning a visit from my goddaughter. So, you see, I am offering you the wager before I am sure of my success, and in that way, you cannot claim that I have had an unfair advantage.

Now, dearest. What match shall it be for you? Do say you'll play. First one of us to receive a letter from the other proclaiming a successful match shall own herself to be beat.

I would tell you more of the house party I am arranging to stir the embers of love, but this letter shall cost a fortune to frank as it is. Now you may only imagine the festivities I am planning with games, delicacies, card parties and balls, carols, and all manner of merrymaking. And you must respond in kind to tell me of yours. And, of course, you must believe me to be

Affectionately yours,
Euota Savile

# CHAPTER 2

"Tain-o-bumfit, eddero-bumfit, peddero bumfit, jiggit," Tom Pickles called out as he walked amidst Willelm Armitage's flock of sheep.

Willelm leaned on the gate enclosing the snowy pasture while his newly hired shepherd counted the ewes that were lambing. They all looked to be in good health, which he was pleased to see. When his father was squire, the farmers who cared for the sheep underfed the ewes to cut costs, but it resulted in weaker lambs. Willelm was willing to spend money to have things done correctly.

Tom took off his cap and scratched his head with the rim before calling out to Willelm. "Tha's jiggit-yain o' them."

They had twenty-one ewes that were carrying lambs. The number was still small, but it was increasing. Now that Willelm had acquired additional acreage to pasture the sheep, he was putting more effort into growing his flock. He hoped the resulting increase in wool and milk would bring about a greater source of income. He watched the sheep milling about, searching for small patches of grass in the pockets where there was no snow, and the sight of his well-tended flock pleased him.

"That's a good number for this year. Bring the ewes that are lambing through the shedder that leads to the smaller barn, and keep them separate. And let me know how Bonnet fares," he added, referring to one of the ewes who was not carrying and who appeared to be ill.

He bid Tom farewell and turned homeward to Lawrence House. There were plenty of other things to do on his land, but Willelm had decided to pay the Saviles a visit in Sharow, where he would deliver his acceptance to Mrs. Savile's Christmas party personally. He had declined to say whether he would stay at Sharow Hall as invited, despite Mrs. Savile's reminder that potential flooding from the River Ure would make daily trips between their houses impossible. Willelm had been in a cynical mood of late and rather thought he would take the risk of floods interrupting their holiday plans and sleep in his own bed.

The groom at Sharow Hall, John Outhwaite, lifted his hand in greeting as he reached for the reins to Willelm's stallion. "'Ow do?"

"Good day to you," Willelm replied. "You're to have a great deal of guests for Christmas. Can you stable all the horses?"

"Aye, we'll be all reet, I reckon," John replied in his ruminative manner.

"I'll let your master know to send word to me if he needs anything."

John nodded, then led the horse to a free stall, and Willelm took the well-worn path to the house. The villages surrounding Ripon were small, and society was tight. He had come to the Saviles' house for visits and parties since childhood, and he knew his way around their rooms as easily as he did his own. He'd often met Juliana here as well, which added charm to his memories, even though he no longer harbored any hopes where she was concerned.

The butler announced him, and Willelm strode into the drawing room, bowing to Mr. Savile and his wife.

"Have a seat," Mr. Savile said—gruffly, to those who didn't know him better. To those who did, his gruffness served as a mask for his sentimental nature and a dislike of its being known.

"I have come to accept your invitation, ma'am," Willelm said, taking the cup of tea prepared to his liking that Mrs. Savile handed him as soon as he was settled. "Thank you for including me. Who else will make up the party?"

Mrs. Savile was seated across from him with a blanket thrown over her legs, and although he had heard she was ailing, there did not seem to be anything amiss. She folded her hands on her lap.

"As far as local families, we will have the Greenwoods, the Taylors, and the Clarks. But I don't suppose that is what you really wish to know," she said with a glimmer of a smile. "You will wish to learn what other young people have accepted, apart from Matthew and Emma."

Willelm did wish to know exactly that, but he would not allow his feelings to be so easily read, and he merely nodded.

"Anthony Weld and his sister Clarissa are arriving from London. They are the great-niece and -nephew of a friend of mine, and they wished to celebrate Christmas away from the city, so I extended them an invitation. We will also have Thomas Sutcliffe and his cousin Margery White from York. You must surely remember them. And Juliana Issot has been invited as well."

Despite Willelm's best intentions to remain indifferent, his throat went dry at the sound of Juliana's name. He swallowed. "Have they all given their acceptance?"

"They have. I am merely waiting to hear back from the Taylors, but that won't interest you as they have no one your age. As it stands, we'll get up a respectable party of eight young men and women. And with two of the families bringing smaller children, Sharow Hall will be filled with all the merrymaking we could wish for. If everyone gives their acceptance—and I don't see why they should not—our house will hold up to twenty people plus their servants."

*Juliana is coming.* Willelm was still trying to wrap his mind around that fact, as she had until now refused all invitations since removing to London. "We have not had a party like this in Yorkshire for some time."

Mr. Savile set down his empty cup on the table in front of him. "That is because my wife insisted on having her Christmases in London until this year. But I imagine that this is what our Christmas months will be like from here on in as we are not likely to travel in the cold anymore."

Mrs. Savile met her husband's gaze with a mixture of affection—and, Willelm thought, nostalgia—before turning back to him.

"Do you plan to stay at Sharow Hall for the month?" She cocked her head and studied him. "You will say you have too much to do to make such a sacrifice, but please allow me to remind you that finding a wife is also of paramount importance. I know that no young man likes to be reminded of such a thing, but it is nevertheless the truth."

Willelm shifted in his seat and crossed one leg over the other. "I, uh…"

"I am not saying you will find your wife amongst the four women who will be staying here, but perhaps it might lead to other invitations and other young women."

Mrs. Savile sipped her tea, her eyes lit with what he could only describe in his current mood as calculation.

"You must allow me to act in the way of a mother to you since yours is no longer with us. Your one London Season did not prove fruitful, Willelm, and you must not think there is no more to be done on your part. Wives do not generally fall into the laps of their husbands without a little effort on the man's part."

Mr. Savile laughed. "*Most* wives don't fall into the laps of their husbands, but might I remind you, my love, that that is precisely how we met?"

Mrs. Savile sent her husband an exasperated look, which was accompanied by a blush. Willelm had not thought a woman her age could still do such a thing.

"Yes, I have always been clumsy, and you need not remind me, Mr. Savile. However, most young women are not so and require a chase." She turned back to Willelm. "You need to make a bit of effort if you wish to succeed in finding a wife."

Despite the fact that Willelm was in perfect agreement with everything Mrs. Savile said, he did not like having his hand forced. Had it been anyone less worthy of his respect, he would have been tempted to raise his hackles and respond that he was perfectly capable of finding his own wife, thank you very much.

But to do so to Mrs. Savile would not only be rude, it would be a falsehood. The truth was, tucked away here in Yorkshire and meeting the same families as he always was, his probability of finding a wife who suited him in every particular was not high. Willelm was pleased to hear that Mr. Sutcliffe and Miss White would be joining the party, for he had not seen them in a number of years. And then there was the addition of Miss Weld, who might prove to be a prospect. As for the local families who made up the guests, Emma Greenwood was a pleasant enough girl, although she did not set his fancy on fire.

Juliana Issot, on the other hand...she simply could not be listed in the same breath as the others as a prospect or a diversion. She was too unique and too special to him. They had shared a real friendship. In fact, she had only just reached her majority when he had decided that she suited him in every particular—except for the one where she would not have him.

As if Mrs. Savile had read his mind, she asked, "How long has it been since you've seen Juliana?"

Willelm pretended to think, although he knew precisely how

long it had been. It was a couple of months shy of two years since he had seen her at their last joint London party, and she had barely given him more than a nod. Oh, she had been perfectly friendly, but his intention to travel to London with the specific object of wooing her had not gone precisely as planned.

In their youth, he and Juliana had ridden to the hounds together, had played together, had been perfectly friendly—and had never entertained a thought about love. It was when Willelm reached his twenty-fourth year that he had decided it was time to settle down. And from the moment he had come to that rational conclusion, he had been struck by the slowly dawning realization that none other than Juliana Issot would suit. She was five years younger than him, but that did not weigh with him when their friendship had been carried out on such equal terms. As a child, Juliana had been less like a young lady in training and more like a scamp. With time, she had grown into an attractive young woman, and her playful, intrepid spirit that she brought to their friendship had only added to her charms.

So he had gone about courting her the same way he did everything. He laid out a plan, he rented a lodging in London, he looked up some of his Cambridge friends who were there, and he got himself invited to all the places where she might be. It was an excellent plan, and Willelm still could not believe it had borne no fruit.

He had certainly expected that Juliana would entertain him as a suitor, even giving him a prominent place—reminiscing about all the memories they'd shared. Instead, she had given him the right-about and made him to understand she did not wish for a stolid Yorkshireman but wanted distinguished suitors who led exciting lives—and likely possessed greater inheritances. He had returned to Yorkshire disillusioned, and now he wondered when she arrived whether he would find the

Juliana of Yorkshire or the Miss Issot of London. Was there anything left in her of his old friend?

Willelm came out of his black study when he noticed both the Saviles looking at him in expectation. He uncrossed his legs and sat up. "I'm sorry, what were we saying?"

"I had asked when the last time was you saw Juliana," Mrs. Savile said, her gaze shrewd.

"Oh." Willelm cleared his throat. "Forgive me for not answering. Juliana and I have not seen each other these two years past. I had...been thinking about the conversation with Tom Pickles this morning about the state of my flock. "

"The very definition of wool-gathering, is that not so?" Mr. Savile said with a chuckle.

Willelm could not help but laugh. "Precisely."

He needed to return an answer about whether or not he would stay at Sharow Hall. As much as he wished to remove himself from all matchmaking schemes, he knew that Mrs. Savile had the right of it. It was time to focus his efforts back on finding a wife.

"To respond to your invitation more fully, Mrs. Savile, I would be delighted to stay here for the month of Christmas. It is true that the river puts our house party at risk. Thank you for your invitation."

"Delightful!" Mrs. Savile clapped her hands together and shot her husband a knowing look that made Willelm wonder how much scheming she had already done.

Mr. Savile beamed. "You will add to the gaiety of our party."

"Surely not, sir," Willelm answered, allowing himself a wry expression. "As you know, I am of too phlegmatic a nature to do any such thing."

Mr. Savile chuckled and stroked his beard. "So you say. But there is a hidden vein of humor underneath that serious exterior. And someone is going to coax it out one day. After you finish your tea, let us go out to the stable, and I will show you the broodmare I've bought. I think you will be impressed."

The topic of horses was always one that interested Willelm, and it was safer than matrimony. "Willingly."

# CHAPTER 3

Juliana broke her journey to Yorkshire with four nights spent at posting inns, where Betty made up the beds with sheets they had brought from home. She allowed Hazel to sniff around at their temporary lodgings and exercise her fidgets. Only her dog's advanced age had allowed Juliana to envision a journey by stagecoach with Hazel in accompaniment.

They pulled into Ripon on the fifth day, and the stagecoach blew the horn loudly to announce their arrival. Juliana shifted in her seat, cold and stiff from traveling, as the coach lumbered into the center of town and came to a stop. The door to the stagecoach opened, and she took a cautious step out, her dog held firmly in one hand and her muff in the other. Betty followed behind.

The streets were thronged with people, and two factory boys walked directly in front of Juliana in animated chatter. One with ears that stuck out from underneath his cap punched one hand into the other for the benefit of his friend as he boasted, "Ah fotched 'im such a claht." A woman on the opposite side of the street sold pork pies from a table in front of her shop and called out, "Growlers! Kessmass stand pies." A driver to her right shouted, "Heyt!" and Juliana took a step back as his carriage moved forward, sending a piece of icy mud onto her cloak.

She bent down and released Hazel from her grasp. The terrier stretched her front legs forward but remained at her mistress's side. The street was dark with frozen mud and sparse clumps of snow partially melted. Through the crowds of people and bustle of carriages, Juliana could discern none belonging to her godmother. It did not overly concern her. In the unlikely event that she had been forgotten, the people at the inn on the side of the road would assist her in any way she needed. *These are my people*—a thought that was as surprising as it was sudden.

"Miss, isn't that the gentleman as came to see you in London?" Betty pointed to a smart coach approaching, with two men on the box seat, led by horses that would have been the envy of any London gentleman. Juliana was momentarily blinded by the sun at the driver's back and could not see anything other than his form, which reminded her of...

"Juliana!"

Willelm Armitage came into view, wearing the rare, broad smile Juliana remembered of her old friend. She had not seen that smile even once on his face when they'd met in London. The fact that he was glad to see her now touched her, and she returned his smile as she lifted her face up to him. He had grown somehow in the two years since she had seen him. Perhaps not in height, but in distinction. There was a firmness to his mouth that showed resolution, and all signs of boyishness were gone. The change became him.

"Willelm!" she called out, grasping her reticule and muff in her two hands. "Are you here by chance or did my godmother send you?"

He handed his reins to the groom who sat beside him and swung down next to her. Hazel barked, and Willelm looked down. "You're here, are you?" He reached his hand down, and Hazel licked it with slavish adoration.

"I never could understand why she adores you so much," Juliana said with a mix of teasing and affection.

"Could you not?" he replied, addressing Hazel. Then he straightened and, as if in afterthought, bowed. "Mrs. Savile sent me, but I was very glad to be of use. I was hoping you might not have forgotten me completely."

Juliana laughed as he had meant for her to do, but there was a twinge of guilt that plagued her. She had not treated him as kindly as she should have done when they had met in London. But the Season was for sampling all forms of gaiety—within proper bounds, of course—and for partaking in all that was new. She had wanted to throw off everything that reminded her of home and mingle with the most dazzling acquaintances attending the brightest parties. Willelm had been too staid and sober to keep pace with glittering London society, and it had not been difficult to choose other, more interesting company.

"I could never forget an old friend," she replied, shutting her mouth before she could do something so foolish as to offer an apology for her behavior toward him in London. That was better forgotten, and it did not seem he expected one. Willelm was a dear friend, but she did not wish to give him the wrong impression that she was now angling for a deeper connection. Although at times it had crossed her mind that perhaps he was.

"Excellent." He took a breath, then gestured toward his coach. "I have my groom with me, whom I believe you remember."

The groom lifted his cap. "Nah then, lass."

"Good day, Joseph. How are you?" Juliana grinned at the weathered Yorkshireman she had known from birth. He had seen her in more than a few scrapes and had never batted an eye.

"Fair t'middlin', I thank 'ee."

Turning to Willelm, Juliana said, "Well, we shall travel in style. What fine horses you have. After five days on the road traveling by stagecoach, this will be a treat indeed."

Willelm studied her for a moment, and she wished she could read his expression. She realized she had missed him.

He turned to his groom, breaking the gaze. "Joseph, give me those reins, and go and see that Miss Issot's trunk is taken care of."

The groom hurried off to do as he was told, and Betty murmured that she would make sure he had the right one.

"There are to be more than twenty of us at the Saviles', I believe," Willelm said as he opened the door to the coach and let down the step. "Up with you, Hazel." He lifted the dog gently and placed her on the floor of the carriage, where she settled in.

Juliana's eyes widened. "Us! Will you make up the number at Sharow Hall? Or perhaps you only meant that you will stay at Lawrence House and come from time to time."

Willelm looked almost sheepish when he answered. "I suppose I could have remained at Lawrence House. But Mrs. Savile desired for me to stay at Sharow and make up the party. She was afraid that potential flooding would interrupt my participation—as it surely would have done had we had this party last year. She did not wish to take the risk, and neither did I."

Juliana brightened at the idea of spending a month with her friend. Perhaps it would not be so onerous to be tucked away in Yorkshire, far from London and all the excitement that was to be found there. It was a pity that Caroline had at last invited her for Christmas *after* Juliana had sent her acceptance letter to her godmother, but she would not think of that. She and Willelm were sure to pick their friendship up where they had left off, and the Saviles would provide some of the Christmas games and traditions Juliana had enjoyed in her childhood. Her mother had been right in saying there was no Christmas like one spent in Yorkshire.

The maid and groom returned, with Joseph carrying the trunk and Betty bringing her own affairs and Juliana's portmanteau. She helped the groom attach the belongings to the back of the carriage.

Willelm lifted his hand to help Juliana into the coach, then assisted her maid. "Let us not delay in getting you to Sharow Hall, which will be as warm as it is comfortable. Everyone eagerly awaits your arrival and will be all too glad to see you." Willelm climbed in himself and took the seat next to Juliana. He tapped on the roof, and they were off.

It was less than two miles to their destination, and as the carriage rumbled forward, Juliana turned to Willelm. "I was sorry to hear about your father. I wished to write to you my condolences, but my mother reminded me that one does not write to gentlemen, even ones who are old friends. And now you are Squire."

"Now I am Squire," he repeated. He paused and looked at her curiously. "Did you really wish to write to me?"

"Of course." Juliana knit her brows, then looked down at her gloves. She wanted to reproach him for doubting her friendship, but one thought to how she had treated him in London was all it took for her to see that any indignation coming from her would not carry weight. She knew Willelm had not had the easiest time with his father and that his loss must be a mixed affair. It made her regret even more that she had not been able to be there for him. His mother's death five years earlier had been that much harder, but at least she had been in Yorkshire.

Juliana drew in a deep breath. "And who else will be part of the Christmas party this year?"

Willelm listed the guests, adding, "The Greenwoods have already arrived, as have the Clarks and the Taylors. Anthony and Clarissa Weld—brother and sister from London—are expected later today. I believe we will be complete at the week's end when Thomas Sutcliffe and Margery White arrive from York."

"That is all most agreeable, but the Welds? How odd that they should be acquainted with my godmother."

Willelm returned no answer, and Juliana was left to wonder to what purpose they had been invited.

Clarissa Weld was everything Juliana admired in society, and she was astonished that she would agree to a sojourn in the wilds of Yorkshire. In fact, Juliana had difficulty imagining Clarissa anywhere but London. Delicate, with hair so blonde it was nearer to white, she had the appearance of an angel. Her words were chosen with care, and when she spoke in her quiet voice, men and women alike hushed to catch her words. Her brother was as dark as she was fair, and there was also more color to his personality. Had they been invited for the potential of making a match with one of the guests?

It was clear enough that Clarissa would not suit Willelm, although it was high time he settled down and found a wife. It was not in Willelm's nature to be frivolous. However, Juliana had difficulty imagining him with any young woman—much less Miss Weld—at his side, despite the obvious lack of reasoning behind such logic.

If Juliana's godmother had included Mr. Weld with a thought for her, then she could only be grateful. He might potentially make a desirable suitor. She had crossed paths with him in London in the past, and he was not displeasing to look at. His family was well respected. She could not be sure whether he was the eldest son, but their London house was said to be in a desirable location. Juliana's lips lifted at the thought, and she turned her considering gaze to Willelm. Perhaps the month might not be wasted, and there would be something to this Christmas party after all.

The carriage rolled to a stop in the sweeping drive of

Sharow Hall, and Raynold Savile waved aside his butler and exited the house at their arrival. Willelm helped Juliana out of the stagecoach, and she stood on the gravel, breathing in as she looked up at the hall she had not visited for three years. It was a beautifully proportioned brick structure with windows lining its two main wings, which held sixteen bedrooms. Juliana knew the inside of each and every one, and she grew cheerful at the thought of placing her trunk in the one she knew would be hers: the yellow room still decorated in the Georgian style, whose wall hangings boasted an oriental design. As a child, she had thought the red dragons magnificent.

Mr. Savile came over and gave her a kiss on the cheek. "Welcome, welcome," he said, taking her by the arm and leading her toward the house. "You brought Hazel, did you? I told Euota you would."

"And how is my godmother?" Juliana asked, her heart light at having finally arrived. Her maid bustled behind her to point out their belongings to the footman who had descended the steps to help.

"She is as pleased as can be to have her guests begin to arrive, most particularly you. She has not stopped to rest these past two weeks," he replied, leaving Juliana in a state of perplexity.

"I was to understand that my godmother was very unwell," she replied with hesitation.

"Oh, she had a sore foot and cannot walk about as much she would like. But otherwise, she is in fine fettle."

This fact was confirmed for Juliana directly when she came into the drawing room where Mrs. Savile was seated. Her complexion was rosy, and the way she clasped her hands and beamed up at Juliana showed her to be the picture of health. Juliana wanted to take her to task for having dissembled, but she was disarmed under her godmother's benevolent smile.

The greeting was interrupted by a growl at Juliana's side as

Hazel took exception to the bulldog sitting at the feet of her godmother's sofa.

"Oh, you have a puppy," she exclaimed above the racket of both dogs barking and growling. "What a dear he is."

"This rascal is Pom," Mrs. Savile said, reaching down to pet her dog and telling him to shush.

Willelm gestured to Hazel with a sharp command—"Quiet!" —and the terrier's bark dissolved into a whimper as she lay at Juliana's feet.

Juliana put her hand on her hip and turned to Willelm. "My dog obeys you better than she does me, and I do not know whether to be pleased or annoyed."

Willelm only grinned at her in response, and the memory of who he was in Yorkshire came back in full force. If he had not shown to his advantage in London, in Yorkshire, Willelm Armitage was respected by men and animals alike.

"Forgive me for not getting up, my dear," Mrs. Savile said. "I fear I am quite crippled in one foot from a piece of carelessness."

Juliana came and sat beside her godmother, giving her a kiss on the cheek. "When you wrote to my mother, your health seemed in some peril."

"Oh heavens, is that so?" Mrs. Savile replied with a guilty chuckle. "I may have exaggerated a tiny bit just to get a glimpse of you this Christmas. But I knew you would forgive me when you remembered how much you liked being here. Was it very wrong?"

Juliana pressed her lips together with mock severity. "It would serve you right if I were to take the first stagecoach back to London, ma'am. But the truth is, I cannot bear the thought of getting bounced about in a stagecoach for at least another month, so I shall have to stay. Willelm has been telling me about all the entertainment we are to have."

Willelm had remained at the entrance to the drawing room,

and Mrs. Savile called out to him. "Will you check the billiard room and see if Matthew Clark is there? He was looking for you and said he would be glad for a game if you could give him one."

"Certainly," Willelm said and left the room.

Juliana turned back to her godmother, who reached over and patted her leg. "Was your trip from Ripon comfortable?"

"Vastly better than the stagecoach," Juliana replied, reaching up to remove her velvet bonnet. "Even if my parents would not have traveled by stagecoach, it is a long journey, and I can understand their reluctance to make it. It was a pleasant surprise in Ripon to find Willelm there to greet me."

"I knew I was right to send him, especially since he is such an old friend of yours. How long has it been since you've seen each other?" Mrs. Savile lifted her eyes and wrinkled her nose as if searching her memory. Her expression made her look younger than her years.

"About two years," Juliana replied. That fact was rather remarkable, considering how close they had been while she had lived in Yorkshire.

"Well, you will have this month to catch up. And now that it is just the two of us, I can give you your gift for St. Nicholas's Day."

Juliana looked down in surprise at the box her godmother handed her, which had been kept tucked at her side.

"Oh no," Juliana exclaimed, her voice soft as she took it. "That is too kind of you." She lifted the lid of the square velvet box the size of her palm, and inside found a gold necklace that had a pendant in the shape of a horseshoe. On the bottom of the horseshoe were six sapphire stones. Her admiration came out in a sigh. "It's the horseshoe that we hang on the door for Christmas, isn't it?"

Her godmother nodded, looking pleased. "Six nails to hold it up for the first six days of Christmas, and six nails to remove for the last days until Twelfth Night. And the horseshoe holds all the good luck for the coming year. May this party bring you luck that will last well into the new year."

Now truly touched, Juliana put her arms around her godmother. "Thank you. I shall treasure it."

Once she had had her tea, Juliana was sent on her way to freshen up in the Georgian bedroom that was to be hers for the month. Her footsteps echoed on the wood floors as she crossed the corridor, with Hazel's nails making scratching sounds as she scurried past. Juliana crossed over to the stairwell in the middle of the great hall and walked to the first landing, where she paused and looked through the window. On the ledge, there was the great porcelain planter with ram's heads she had hid behind as a girl when playing hide and seek.

She picked up Hazel and walked the rest of the way upstairs, then traveled down the familiar silk rug in the corridor that led to her room. She opened the door to her bedroom and set Hazel on the floor, and the dog immediately went over to the bed and dove under it, sniffing. The curtains on the window and matching bedspread had been replaced with something lighter in color, with a subtle pattern of light green fronds on gold.

"Oh, look at this," she told Hazel. "The dragons are gone." She experienced a flash of disappointment that her old Yorkshire room, that was reserved for her whenever she visited her godmother, had been brought into fashion. She had rather liked its old charm.

Juliana went over to the desk and touched the paper left there, her thoughts turning to the visitors that were to arrive— the Welds, Thomas and Margery, whom she had not seen in ages. And although it was easy to do so, she must not forget about Matthew and Emma. Juliana then went and sat before the fire, patting her lap for Hazel to climb up. She stroked her ears absently, wondering what pleasures this month might hold.

# CHAPTER 4

W illelm did not find Matthew in the billiard room and decided to abandon the quest. He walked over to the window and contemplated the snowy landscape before turning and picking up the cue and placing the balls on the table. He stood, slender cue in hand, and stared at the balls until his vision blurred and their forms blended together.

His heart rate had remained steady in Juliana's presence, which was a promising sign that he would be in command of himself. He'd been eager to see her but was not in any sort of mood to play the lovesick fool. He almost despised himself for thinking of her in that context at all. Really, she should remain firmly in the place of his childhood friend and nothing more. She had certainly never asked for anything more.

At the same time, there was something about Juliana that was unlike anyone else, and he found he couldn't place her in any category at all. As soon as he saw her again, he knew that in essentials she had not changed, despite the years and despite London. She had the capacity to listen as though there was nothing more important in the world in that moment than him.

When it was just the two of them, he had told her things about his father that he had never shared with anyone else, and her responses, measured and wise for her age, had never failed to soothe him. Willelm knew his own mind. He was woven with loyal fibers, and once he had confided his heart to one woman, it was hard to think of opening himself up to anyone else in that way.

He took position and eyed the ball with the cue stretched back. The colored balls scattered with a loud *crack*. He must keep an open mind where his heart was concerned, however. Mrs. Savile had taken great pains to bring new society to their Yorkshire party. He would have a chance to meet two young women, one of whom he had known only as a child and the other of whom he had never met. And he would become better acquainted with Emma Greenwood, who was familiar. Perhaps one of these women would suit.

Willelm played for an hour in perfect silence, and when he had played enough, cast off an impulse to ride home and visit his estate. Lord Darlington had given him permission to host a fox hunt on his own land as long as it did not conflict with the Raby Hunt. Willelm had arranged matters with the Saviles, and his fox hunt would be included in their Christmas festivities. He wanted to ride over the lands with a mind to the hunt, but he resisted. He had promised to make up one of the party, so he would do what the other guests did for this month, which meant remaining at Sharow Estate.

He spent a somewhat insipid afternoon, where he did not cross paths with Juliana or any of the other guests, and he hoped this was not a glimpse of what was in store for the entire month. Sounds of the Welds' arrival did not reach him until later in the day when he had already retired to his room to dress for dinner. He would have to wait to make their acquaintance.

Willelm possessed no valet but had little difficulty in seeing to it that he was correctly attired in breeches and silk stockings before he made his way downstairs. The Saviles came from a different era, and dressing for dinner was important to them. The drawing room was empty, save Juliana, and she turned from the fireplace to greet him, her mouth lifting at the sight of him. She wore a becoming ivory gown with a low neckline. It was edged with ivory lace, which gave slightly more coverage to her bodice.

"You look very fine, Jules," he said as he bowed over her hand. She rewarded him with a broader smile that brought out her dimples.

"Do you like the gift my godmother gave me?" She pointed to her necklace, and it was small enough that he had to draw near to see it. That move was perhaps not the wisest because it flooded him with a sudden awareness of her female attractions. He caught a whiff of her sweet perfume and a close-up glance at the creamy skin on her neck before he stepped back abruptly.

"Is that...is that a horseshoe?" He managed to get the question out after clearing his throat, fearing he sounded like an idiot tripping over his own words. But honestly—what did she expect to accomplish, leaning forward in such a way?

"It is." Her friendly grin showed how singularly unaware she was of the effect she had on him. "Do you catch its significance?"

Willelm searched his mind for what she could mean but came up blank. Then again, his mind did not seem to be working properly at the moment. "Mrs. Savile knows you like horses?"

"No, silly. It's the Christmas horseshoe that we hang on our doors in Yorkshire. To tell the truth, I am looking forward to all the decorating. I wish we might start now."

"Oh, of course." Willelm was still feeling unsettled and slightly foolish. By sheer will, he forced himself to attend to the conversation. "There will be the games, of course. And those we can start as early as tonight."

Her eyes lit at the suggestion. "True! We must be sure to propose it."

They drew a breath and pointed at each other in unison as they exclaimed, "Bullet pudding!" before dissolving into laughter. One of his favorite Christmas memories of Juliana was the year they had played that game—both of them fiercely competitive— but she had had the ill luck to cut the pile of flour in such a way as to cause the bullet to fall from its summit. Juliana had then had to fish it out with her teeth. He chuckled again, remembering how covered in flour she had been. It was all over her face, with only her eyes, nostrils, and teeth spared by the white powder. It had even been dusted through the curls that sprang out next to her forehead. It was one of those rare occasions when she did not look absolutely perfect. He had liked her even more for it.

The door opened, and the Welds stepped into the room. It had not taken them long to dress for dinner despite arriving late. Mr. Weld was the perfect specimen of a London Corinthian. Handsome, tall—something Willem could not claim to possess—with a decided air of fashion. He was just the sort of man who had flocked around Juliana in her London Season, and Willelm's sense of irritation grew that London should invade Yorkshire and compete for Juliana's attention.

"Good evening." Mr. Weld bowed with a flourish over Juliana's hand and threw a careless nod to Willelm, showing that he viewed him as nothing more than a local farmer. It did not take much more than Weld's practiced greeting for Willelm to decide he was a man who always knew what to say, which was another trait Willelm did not possess. In short, he was everything Willelm was not—and, from Juliana's pleased expression, appeared to be everything she desired. The idea of a match being made right under his nose was not an idea Willelm found in the least palatable. He fervently hoped he had not made a mistake in agreeing to stay for the month.

Juliana, however, preened under Weld's attention. "I believe we have met in London. In any case, you are both somewhat known to me through the Renfairs, even if we have not been introduced."

"How do you do?" Miss Weld curtsied to both Willelm and Juliana before her brother could answer. At least Miss Weld treated him with more consideration.

She was perfectly poised and spoke in a well-modulated tone. And, what was more to the point, she was stunning to look at. Where her brother had dark brown hair, hers was pale blonde, and her eyes were large and of the clearest blue he had ever seen. When she turned them on Willelm, he was momentarily mesmerized. She was also more petite than him, which gave him the agreeable sensation of feeling tall. That was not something he regularly experienced.

"Oh yes. Cissy Renfair is a favorite of us both," Mr. Weld replied, breaking the spell his sister had cast over Willelm. "And now we shall have ample time this month to increase our acquaintance, Miss Issot, which I look forward to."

Miss Weld turned to address Juliana. "And did you not attend the Jarveys' rout? I believe we may have been sitting at the supper table near to one another. I recognize your red curls."

Willelm knew that while Juliana liked her red hair, she did not like comments made about it. Her polite expression spoke volumes even without the dry tone used in her response.

"Everyone remembers my curls."

Mrs. Savile entered the room, leaning heavily on a cane and relying on the assistance of her husband. It was clear her foot was still paining her. The Yorkshire families came in behind them without their younger children, who would be eating in the schoolroom. Willelm shook hands with Matthew and bowed before Emma.

The footmen opened the door that led to the dining room, and Mr. Savile gestured his guests forward. "Let us not stand on ceremony. Please, find whatever seat at the table suits you." He assisted his wife into the room, where he placed her at the foot of the table. Willelm rushed to the center and outbid Mr. Weld in taking the seat at Juliana's side, and Weld was forced to sit by Emma Greenwood.

"We will be dining *à la russe* this evening," Mrs. Savile said from her place at the table. As soon as she finished speaking, an array of servants came in bearing an identical dish for each person and placed it in front of them.

The first course was white soup, an old warming favorite. Willelm had no siblings and no family left, and he rarely entertained. He inhaled the scent of the salted, creamy broth. If little else came out of this month's party, it would be nice to have the festive foods. He was not likely to have gone to such trouble just for himself.

Juliana picked up her spoon and dipped it into the soup, taking a small, silent sip. "Delicious. I've missed the Saviles' cook's way of preparing it."

"What would you have done this Christmas if you had not come here?" he asked. "To tell the truth, it's been so long since I've seen you I hardly know what occupies your attention anymore. In some ways I feel like I hardly know you now."

A brief frown flashed over Juliana's face before she rearranged her features. "This is heavy conversation for the dinner table," she said, a forced lightness to her tone.

She was right. Willelm had never been at ease in social settings and was not interested in "doing the pretty," as his London friends called it. He would rather get right to the heart of it and talk about what truly mattered. However, even he could see his comment was gauche. At this rate, not only would he never win Juliana's heart, he was not likely to win anyone's.

"I apologize." He risked a quick touch on her hand, then covered it up by handing her the salt cellar. "You know me well enough to know that I am not skilled at idle chatter."

She smiled. "I do know that, but I also know you have a host of other strengths. You're an excellent horseman, you practice husbandry, and you always say precisely what you think, and that is something to value. And you're the most loyal friend a person could wish for."

Willelm was stunned. He had not expected such a litany of compliments. He had almost thought she had completely forgotten who he was.

Juliana went on. "To answer your question, I was invited to Caroline Fulham's house for Christmas, and I would have gone had her invitation come before my godmother's. As fate would have it, I had already sent off my acceptance when Caroline's invitation came at last. And so it was too late." She leaned in to whisper, "I would not admit to anyone but you that this was not my first choice, and I beg you to keep it to yourself."

Willelm nodded and could only be thankful that Mrs. Savile's invitation had arrived before Miss Fulham's had. Perhaps there was hope for him yet. Surely fate would not toy with him in such a way by bringing Juliana back to Yorkshire only to have her fly off again? He leaned back as the servants lifted their soup dishes from in front of the guests, some barely touched and others scraped clean. He had managed to finish his soup. He did not precisely overindulge at the table, but he did not like waste, and this was a very good soup.

"I am sure it is not what you would wish to hear, but I must tell you how pleased I am that you accepted *this* invitation instead of that one. I may not have you for much longer, for it seems as though your future is to be in London. But I should like to have this one last month with my old friend before you're gone forever."

He did not turn to see Juliana's expression to his candid words—words he could not have held back even if he tried. The servants came and set in front of them plates of quail with sides of cauliflower buds braised in butter. Without risking a glance at his dinner partner, he picked up his fork and knife and began the second course.

# CHAPTER 5

Juliana chewed her food mechanically. Willelm's words had brought forth an unexpected sadness, although he'd said no less than the truth. All her plans revolved around the idea of residing in London, marrying a member of the *ton*, and remaining there. If she thought about returning to Yorkshire at all, it was only in the vaguest of terms to satisfy any nostalgic urge that might come upon her. She certainly did not envision making her home here.

Therefore, what a surprise it was to find that the Yorkshire spirit had not left her so easily. While she and Betty had been unpacking, the scullery maid had hurried into Juliana's room with apologies for interrupting her and promises to "fettle" the fire. Betty had glanced at her in confusion, but the maid's language was perfectly comprehensible to Juliana. In fact, as soon as she had stepped out of the stagecoach in Ripon, the broad Yorkshire accents had struck her as colorful and familiar. And then there were the snow-covered meadows, separated by low stone walls easily distinguishable through the stagecoach window. It was all so much a part of her, she could not imagine cutting Yorkshire completely out of her life. If only she could have the comfort of Hutton Conyers in the much more exciting city of London, where people wore fine dresses and attended fancy balls, and a bit of novelty was more likely to happen to a person.

And now with Willelm hinting that he would not be seeing her anymore? That had stung, although she supposed she deserved it. She had scarcely exchanged two words with him in London and had not come back to visit Yorkshire since. Nor had she sent him word when Emma Greenwood had left London after only one Season, which would have been a basic courtesy. Juliana wondered if the thought of her not being in Willelm's life made him sad as well. Perhaps just a bit since the words "gone forever" had sounded mournful.

Mrs. Savile had not been joking when she said they'd be dining *à la russe*. They had every one of the fourteen dishes brought out to them in succession. After the seventh dish, Juliana could barely fit any more food in and only made a show of eating the delicacies. It mattered little, as she knew her godmother would not waste anything. Whatever could not be turned into a dish for another meal, the servants would partake of. There was not a servant among the Saviles' who would entertain the thought of leaving Sharow Hall.

Matthew Clark sat at the table on Juliana's other side. He had grown into a tall, wiry man whose pale skin made a show at sprouting whiskers, but those were sparse. He seemed to be as uncomplicated a man as he'd been a boy, for all that he was a gentleman. He reminded her of Willelm in his simplicity, his sports-mad tendencies, and his appreciation of country life. One might almost lump him into the same mold as Willelm, except that her friendship with Matthew did not go beyond the superficial. With Willelm, it was different.

Matthew lifted his eyes from his plate and found her looking at him. He indicated the slice of cheese with his knife. "This is from a Swaledale sheep. They had it brought in specially."

"Oh." Juliana looked at the cheese in question, which resembled...cheese, then she glanced back at him. The conversation did not flourish after that, and Matthew went back to eating.

Perhaps he was not so very much like Willelm after all. As much as Juliana had thought Willelm simple, he needed only a comparison with Matthew to bring out his layers of complexity. Willelm had the element of surprise. Just when she thought he would rip at her for being thoughtless, as she'd surely deserved, he would be surprisingly tender and full of grace. And just when she thought she could twist him around her finger, he proved inexplicably obstinate. Willelm was perhaps not so much simple as he was genuine.

Juliana looked up when she realized that in comparing the two gentlemen on either side of her, she was neglecting both. Mr. Weld had his eyes on her from across the table, and he smiled when she met his gaze. She returned it, but flushed at having allowed herself to daydream.

Willelm leaned in to her and murmured in barely audible tones, "The cheese on your plate that you are *not* eating is from a Swaledale."

"I know—" she began, looking up to meet his gaze, and bit her lip when she saw his laughing eyes. He had been following Matthew's attempt at conversation. "Beast," she returned, without heat.

At the end of the fourteen courses, Mr. Savile assisted his wife to her feet. "Gentlemen, I shall join you in a moment. As you can see, my wife—strong though she is—could do with a little assistance until she is fully mended."

The gentleman stood, and Juliana followed the ladies into the drawing room, wishing she could have spent more time talking to Willelm. Emma fell into step beside her. She had grown up in the same circle as Juliana but lacked the excitement to attract Juliana as a close friend. Just the fact that she wasn't interested in more than one Season seemed proof enough of her unsuitability for the role, if any were needed.

Emma nodded to Miss Weld, who walked in at Mrs. Clark's side before turning back to Juliana. "I was surprised to hear that you would make up the party. I had almost thought you would not return to Yorkshire again."

The comment irritated Juliana, coming from someone other than Willelm. She frowned at Emma. "Why should I not return? This is my home as well as yours."

Emma shrugged. They entered the drawing room, and she took a seat next to Juliana. Mrs. Clark joined the other ladies of a certain age on the far side of the drawing room, and Emma gestured for Miss Weld to join them before answering.

"I returned to Hutton Conyers after one London Season, although, like you, I could have chosen to stay since my aunt has her home there. But I hope to marry a Yorkshireman, myself." She brushed her thin, white hands along her dress. "Let us just say that I've not seen the same desire in you—a sentiment I can sympathize with, although I don't share it."

Juliana softened. Emma was not trying to infuse disapproval into everything she said as she'd thought. Perhaps Juliana had been too much accustomed to the ways of society to remember that not everything needed to be a competition. However, it did not change the fact that she and Emma had little in common. Between her and Matthew, who could not be counted upon to liven any conversation, Juliana was beginning to remember why she had been so anxious to escape local company.

"I have had much to keep me occupied in London, it is true. But you shall see just how content I am to be here." She smiled at Miss Weld, anxious that she should be included. "Miss Weld, I hope you will also enjoy your stay here."

"I'm sure I shall." Miss Weld returned the smile, but it seemed as forced and polite as her own had been. Juliana hoped a warmer relationship might grow between the women.

Mrs. Greenwood, Mrs. Taylor, and Mrs. Clark were in discussion with Juliana's godmother in the chairs placed on the other end of the room, and Mrs. Savile now clapped her hands and called the younger women over.

"We have a month to amuse ourselves, and although Mr. Savile and I have discussed ideas amongst ourselves, we want to know what sorts of things you wish to do this holiday. We don't want anyone to leave disappointed."

"Of course, we shall have to have snapdragon for the children," Emma said. Her younger sisters—Ann and Mary, who were six and nine—also made up the party, although they had remained with their governess in the schoolroom for dinner.

"And snapdragon for us," Juliana said, grinning in anticipation of snatching the tasty raisins out of the flaming brandy stew. She was rewarded for her contribution by a nod of agreement from her godmother.

"I would like to sing Christmas carols," Miss Weld replied, surprising Juliana. She hadn't expected her to request something so simple and…pure. Miss Weld flushed as though self-conscious at her admission. "They make me nostalgic. I hope I will know the words to the songs you have here."

"An excellent idea," Mrs. Savile said. "There must always be Christmas carols for a proper celebration. I own a preference to 'God Rest You Merry, Gentlemen', myself. It's so cheering."

"That one is my very favorite," Miss Weld replied.

"And 'Deck the Halls,'" Juliana added. "We can sing it while we string up ivy."

They continued with other ideas that included a variety of card games, along with the more riotous games of hot cockles and hoodman's blind. Before long, the gentleman returned from sharing the port and gathered around the ladies, who were sitting in a larger circle. Mr. Weld came straight for Juliana and took the place next to her that Emma had vacated to bring a cup of tea to her mother.

Mr. Savile stood at his wife's side and called everyone's attention. "We are pleased to have nearly all of our guests arrive in time for St. Nicholas's Day to properly open the Christmas season. Mrs. Savile and I wished to tell you of our plans for this month."

Mrs. Savile laid a hand over his. "My dear, we have been discussing this very thing before you arrived. We should have waited for the men."

"Never mind that." His gaze skimmed the assembled crowd. "I am sure our guests can bear with a little repetition. Our stables are open for any riding you might wish to do, and we hope our drawing room will become very merry indeed with Christmas games. Willelm Armitage has graciously invited us all for a fox hunt to be held on his land—is that not so?" He glanced at Willelm, who nodded.

"Which will take place on the nineteenth of December," Mr. Savile continued. "There will be carols, of course, and I hope young Ann and Mary will sing to us on Christmas morning along with little Fanny Taylor. It has been some time since we have heard young voices waking us up for Christmas."

"I am certain Ann and Mary will be delighted," Mr. Greenwood replied.

Mrs. Taylor smiled at the company. "Fanny will do anything Ann and Mary do." Fanny was only five, and she had not remembered Juliana when she had gone to visit the children in the schoolroom. Mary had not either, but Ann had come running as soon as she saw Juliana.

"And we will rely upon your goodness in making up pretty baskets for the St. Thomas widows, as well as tying up bundles for Boxing Day. We are not standing on ceremony with you, as you are all well-known to us." Mr. Savile caught Anthony Weld's eye. "And I hope Mr. and Miss Weld will count themselves in that number after their stay with us."

"Undoubtedly," Mr. Weld replied, bowing to the company from his seat. Juliana was pleased with his gracious response. He appeared to be perfectly at ease in Yorkshire company.

Mr. Savile continued. "You will discover or rediscover your favorite Yorkshire dishes with so many festive dinners before us. And we will need to elect a first-footer to bring in the New Year. We shall not assume that just because Mr. Weld's hair is black and he is fine to look upon"—at this, everyone laughed—"that he is to be the one. No. This shall be done through a democratic process by way of secret vote. The first-footer task shall go to the most good-natured gentleman among us. For that is what we hope to see more of in the New Year."

Mr. Savile looked down at his wife. "Anything to add, Mrs. Savile?" When she shook her head, he finished by saying, "We will close our Christmas festivities with the Twelfth Night ball. Then we will send everyone back to the monotony of routine and bleak winter weather, where you might bide your days until spring comes to revive us once again."

A round of laughter met Mr. Savile's words, with shouts of encouragement for the proposed plan.

Mrs. Savile looked at her guests. "Why not begin straight away with a card game? Now, what shall we play first?"

"Commerce," someone called out. There was a round of murmured agreement, with no other propositions being put forth.

"Commerce it is." Mrs. Savile signaled to the footman. "Fetch for us a new deck of cards and the chips."

The footman left to do her bidding. A large round table had been set up on the opposite corner of the drawing room in anticipation of the card games, and the guests made their way over to it. It was large enough for the adults, both young and old, to play at the same table.

Juliana sat, expecting Willelm to take a seat on her left as he had always rushed to do when they were younger, but he made no move in her direction, and Mr. Weld took that spot. Instead, Willelm took the last available seat to the right of the dealer. Juliana wondered why he had not wanted to play beside her. Half the fun was guessing how her castoffs might affect his hand.

Matthew Clark dealt three cards to each of the players, and Juliana peeked at her hand. Three queens! She had *never* had a tricorn on the first try. She glanced suspiciously at Matthew. Had he dealt with a preference to her? But he seemed oblivious to her excellent hand. She then looked at Willelm, eager to see his face when he was forced to bow to her triumph. His expression revealed no clues to his own hand or any curiosity about hers.

"Will you buy or trade?" Matthew asked her.

She pursed her lips. "Neither."

On her left, Mr. Weld protested. "Neither! Then you shall not buy or trade at all throughout the entire round. I was looking forward to trading with you. I might even have helped your hand."

"Perhaps I do not need the assistance," she replied with a glimmer of a smile and another glance at Willelm.

Juliana could have ended the game then, knowing how slim the chances were that someone would end up with three kings or three aces, but she allowed the game to go on with buys and trades—laughter and groans, depending on what the players ended up with. She supposed she wanted to prolong the pleasure of her anticipated victory. She peeked at Willelm from around the dealer more than once but could not read any emotion on his face. At last, Miss Weld knocked on the table.

"Show us your hands," Matthew called out.

Juliana went first, biting her lip to keep from smiling. Everyone groaned when they saw her tricorn, and then she could no longer hide her triumph. One by one, the others displayed their hands until they came to Miss Weld, who had knocked to end the game. She had a knave, queen, and king of diamonds. She shrugged and gave a pretty smile. "My loss."

They finished the round of players until they came to Willelm. He did not move until all eyes were on him. Then he peered around Matthew to glance at Juliana as he laid out three aces.

"What!" Everyone exclaimed in shock at his possessing a greater hand than Juliana, and she felt the blood rush to her face. It was only a game. And yet, she did not like surprises, and she did not like to be beaten. He bent his head around Matthew again to look at her, and she caught one of his rare grins. She could not return it.

As the crowd broke up at the end of the game, Juliana went over to stand by the piano, and Willelm came to stand beside her. She pressed her lips together and turned to face him. "You came to gloat."

"Yes," he said, folding his arms, looking smug.

"Well, go gloat in your own corner. I already claimed this one."

"Very well," he replied, but he didn't move.

"I suppose you had a lucky trade, which gave you your remaining ace." Juliana knew her expression was pouting, but she couldn't help herself.

"Two lucky trades, as a matter of fact, and quite early on." Willelm paused as Juliana looked up at him in surprise. "I merely chose to wait until an auspicious moment to display my hand."

"I should have knocked straight away. I would have won." Juliana looked away again, knowing her irritation was exaggerated but unable to explain to herself why she should care. When

Willelm stayed put, she glared at him again and was caught short by his expression. He seemed to be studying her.

"What?" she asked when he remained silent.

Then he leaned in so that his face was close to hers. "Just remember, Jules: As much as you think yourself to be up to snuff, you are not awake upon every suit."

# CHAPTER 6

Willelm pulled off his boots, then stripped off his clothes and donned a nightshirt and cap as he prepared to sleep in the strange bed at Sharow Hall. Despite the fire that had been banked in his room, there was a draught of cold air that slipped under the door. He pulled the covers up to his chin and thought about his conversation with Juliana that had ended with a tightening of her lips and a pulling up of her chin.

She had not liked to see him win—she never had liked losing at anything—but he saw that his words had hit their mark. She might be the belle of London, and she certainly had been while he was there, but she could not have everything upon command. He swung up on one elbow and punched his pillow to create a cradle for his head. *She's certainly not up to snuff on matters of the heart and who would be a good match for her.*

Willelm lay back down with a huff. Visions of the younger version of Juliana flashed through his mind—the girl who had grown over the years in his esteem and affection. Despite their difference in age, she had always been spirited and more mature than her years, even as he was entering adulthood and she was still in the schoolroom. Having lived within a couple of miles of each other, they often sought each other's company at parties, for games—and later, for events such as balls and Christmas festivities. As they were both avid riders, they sometimes met by chance in the countryside on horseback, outside of the annual Raby Hunt. One such ride stood out in Willelm's mind.

He had just buried his mother the week before, and the reality of life without her, living under the slim mercies of a father who was indifferent at best and cruel at worst struck him as unbearable. He had just finished a gallop to clear his mind and was allowing his horse to gain his wind when he spotted Juliana in the distance. He turned his horse in her direction, and she rode toward him, her expression growing tender as she neared.

"I had hoped I would see you." She turned her horse to walk alongside his.

"Where's your groom?" he had asked her.

"I won't bother telling you I don't need one, because you'll just scold as my parents do," she replied. "But what can possibly happen to me here in Studley Gardens?"

"If your parents wish for you to go out with a groom, you must listen to them," he replied. His voice had been severe—his grief had not helped. "You're still just a girl."

"Never mind that." She had tossed her head, and he could still remember her riding bonnet. It had not been in the latest style, but she was growing into such a beauty, she could make stitched-together rags look like something fit for a queen. They rode in silence for some ways before she said, "I had hoped to see you so I could tell you how sorry I was about your mother."

He hadn't answered over the lump in his throat, and she hadn't seemed to expect one. They rode on before he realized he was leading her even farther from her house, and he proposed they turn back. Then he found himself telling her what he had never said to another living soul. "My father is a tyrant."

She nodded. "I thought he might be."

That had surprised Willelm. "So you know? He is so different in company. I didn't think anyone knew. He is so very civil." The bitter words had been choked out of him.

When he looked at Juliana to gauge her response, she gave him a resigned smile. "He is not civil to dogs, and you can always tell a man by the way he treats his animals."

Willelm went silent, but the need to unburden himself had become so great, despite his difficulty in getting the words out. "With my mother's death, I have lost everything that is good in the world. I have no one."

"You have me," she replied, her voice quiet and mature for her sixteen years of age. It was odd how much comfort her words had brought him.

From then on, they had been as inseparable as two friends could be who were not of the same age, nor the same sex, and not quite living next door. It was a fortunate thing Mrs. Issot had insisted on extending her maternal affection to Willelm, because it had provided them with more opportunities to meet. But Mrs. Issot could not force her daughter to entertain Willelm's suit in London, and he had not looked for help in that quarter.

Willelm's pitiful attempt at falling asleep grew nigh impossible when he relived the scene in London where she had called him her "childhood playmate" before sending him off with his tail between his legs. What had happened to turn her from the true friend she had once been to the London Incomparable who spurned good Yorkshire company? Whatever it was, he would not be so foolish as to court her again.

If only he hadn't wanted to drink in the sight of her ever since the stagecoach had rolled into Ripon.

---

On December tenth, the coach carrying Thomas Sutcliffe and Margery White pulled up to the door, bringing the party to its complete number. Mr. Sutcliffe and Miss White were cousins from York, the great-niece and -nephew of Mrs. Savile. In the past, they had traveled north to visit their great-aunt in Sharow, and Willelm knew them enough to call them acquaintances, although their last visit had been eight years ago. What he remembered most was that Thomas was up to any gig proposed, and Margery, a year younger, had already managed a quelling look far in advance of her age that checked their fun.

Before their arrival, Willelm had been in the drawing room, listening to Juliana tease Mr. Weld about his continental air—an offshoot of his Grand Tour, surely—and how it might have become a permanent handicap had Napoleon not escaped his imprisonment, sending all the English home *à toute allure*. Weld had laughed heartily at this sally, and Willelm welcomed the distraction of the new arrivals with relief. It was not as though a man were not a gentleman unless he had done the Grand Tour of the Continent. Willelm frowned. As for himself, if he had not had his Grand Tour, it was because he had had no wish to do so.

Willelm walked past the butler and was the first one outdoors, where he was able to assess Miss White as she exited the carriage. He wasn't entirely sure how to address her, as Juliana and Emma were both friends from childhood, and they had continued with their tradition of using Christian names. Miss Weld was an entirely new acquaintance, and Miss White was known, but they had not frequented each other's company since she had made her debut. He decided to keep to caution and use the formal address.

Eight years had changed Miss White. She could be described as handsome rather than pretty as she had almost the look of a matron, despite possessing a set of ripe lips. Thomas Sutcliffe descended the carriage next and after giving a wave to Willelm, walked over to speak to the coachman.

He looked much the same, except for having acquired a distinguished, *tonnish* air that seemed more suited to London than York. Willelm certainly did not need any more competition for Juliana's attention. The arrival of Anthony Weld had been bad enough in terms of reminding Juliana of all the attractions of London society. When she conversed with Anthony, she appeared more like her London self—colder, somehow. Sutcliffe was also sure to appeal to Juliana with his looks and address. And, as with Mr. Weld, he added height and fortune to his attractions.

*Since when have I been prey to jealousy?* Willelm thought with irritation. It was not in his nature, but he had been battling it since Juliana had arrived. He was determined to be done with so unattractive an emotion. Besides, were they not come in the guise of rivals, he was sure he would have liked both Weld and Sutcliffe.

"Good afternoon, Willelm," Margery said with a smile on those ripe lips. So it was to be *Margery* since she had used his Christian name. "I hope we need not stand on ceremony."

In a rare spurt of chivalry, Willelm bent down to kiss the hand that she had extended to him. "I hope we might not. We are not newly acquainted, after all."

The butler directed the servants to attend to the trunks, and the remaining guests piled out of the house into the brisk air to greet the cousins. Having overheard Margery's words, Anthony said, "Perhaps we might all dispense with formal address if we are to spend nearly a month together."

"I daren't, brother," Miss Weld returned, stepping around from behind Anthony. "At least not with the gentlemen." So it was to be *Miss Weld*.

"Miss Weld!" Thomas called out from where he stood near the coachman. "I had not realized you would be here." When everyone stared at him in surprise, he looked abashed. "We have...already met in London."

Miss Weld's smile became fixed as all eyes swung between her and Thomas, and Juliana stepped into the breach. "If using our Christian names is unpalatable, Miss Weld, you must not do what is uncomfortable. I, for one, do not mind giving the use of my first name with an eye to our particular circumstances. However, perhaps it might be wiser to revert back to formal address when we meet again in London."

*Good,* Willelm thought as a first reaction, but he was torn. On one hand, he preferred that Juliana not make free use of her name with every gentleman. On the other hand, was she really so changeable that she had one set of rules for London and another for Yorkshire?

They had, by this time, all accompanied the new arrivals back into the entryway, and the servants bustled about carrying their trunks and belongings upstairs. Mrs. Savile hobbled forward with her cane and a broad smile. "Wonderful. You are here at last. Now we may truly begin our Christmas festivities. We have a simple afternoon planned, beginning with tea and games. And tomorrow, if you are not too worn out, we have arranged an excursion to Fountains Abbey."

"I have never been," Margery said, "although it had been much talked of on our last visit. It is an open cathedral, I am to understand. Will we not be cold?"

"Bah, I don't care for that," her cousin answered, banishing her objections with a careless grin and glancing once again at Miss Weld. "Of course, we must go."

Willelm had often visited the grounds and ruins of the abbey, of course, but Mrs. Savile had done well to plan this as part of the activities as it was a magnificent site to walk through. An old Cistercian structure dating back to the early twelfth century, Fountains Abbey had once been the most influential of its kind in England, despite the inhospitable surroundings. All that remained was the stone structure and cloisters, and instead of a stone tile floor, there was grass in the summer and snow in the winter. The roof and windows had long since disappeared.

He added his support. "Ladies, you must take care to dress warmly, but I do believe this is a visit you will not want to miss." Willelm wondered if it would bring to Juliana's mind the number of times they had played there when they were younger. Perhaps those memories would stir something in her heart.

There was something pathetic to his longing. He would have preferred to have seen a firmer resolve in himself not to give way to his weakness, since he was fooling himself if he thought he stood a chance. Yet it was not in his nature to give up so easily—not if there was anything of his old Juliana left to win over.

The next day after breakfast, they gathered in the hall for their excursion to Fountains Abbey. Miss Weld appeared stiff in her interactions with Thomas and Matthew, but Willelm had to credit her with being kinder to Juliana and the other young ladies. Perhaps she was simply not at ease with men who were not relations.

A short carriage ride brought them to the site that was familiar to Willelm and Juliana but not to anyone else. As the curve of the road led to the vista that framed the Abbey, Miss Weld looked through the window and lifted her eyes to the ancient structure. "How magnificent."

Willelm was gratified that she could appreciate its beauty. "Wait until you see what is on the inside," he replied as he lifted his hand to help her out of the carriage. Anthony was repeating the process at the other carriage, and he saw a flash of red curls and white teeth as Juliana stepped out. With his eyes on her, he nearly dropped Miss Weld's hand as she leaned on his to alight.

"I'm terribly sorry. Please forgive my clumsiness." Willelm held her hand more firmly. Then, forcing himself to focus on his companion and not dishonor Miss Weld by showing a divided attention, he held out his arm for her to walk next to him. The road was uneven with the frozen ruts left by carriage wheels, and she clung to his side.

"What do you think of Yorkshire so far?" he asked her as the sounds of Emma's cheerful voice and Juliana's low tones reached his ears from where they walked with Anthony and Thomas.

"It is charming, but I must say it is a little cold." Miss Weld had a dainty step and walked slowly, and he was obliged to see Juliana disappearing into the cloisters, now walking beside Thomas.

"Yes, I suppose it is," he replied, reminding himself again to forget Juliana and focus on his current partner. They reached the place where the stone arches held a roof of sky light, and there they turned into the open nave. The others were spread out in the spacious church, and Matthew was leading Margery toward the imposing tower, whose structure remained standing, though its roof and windows were gone.

"I love it here," Willelm said. "The architecture is so simple. It's beautiful, though in ruins."

Miss Weld stopped to look. She let go of his hand so she could spin around to see everything. "Someone should repair it so it might be used again."

"I suppose." Willelm wasn't sure he agreed. He wasn't precisely romantic, but he would miss this place if it were modernized. Besides, he wasn't sure there was enough interest in having an old, out-of-the-way monastery turned into a parish. There would not be enough people in the area to support such a project.

"Help me up!"

Willelm had no problem recognizing Juliana's voice, which rang out behind him in the nave. He turned to see Thomas and Anthony circle back to where Juliana stood, as though she were a magnet. Emma had joined Margery and Matthew on the opposite end of the church.

Juliana held Thomas's hand as she climbed on to a broken pillar in exactly the way she had done when she and Willelm were children. She lifted one arm and extended it, laughing. "Greetings, my loyal subjects."

"Jump, and I will catch you." Anthony moved forward with outstretched hands, and Willelm could see Juliana hesitate. This was also something they had done as children, but indignation rose in his breast at Anthony's command. This was hardly a course of action to encourage a young lady to follow.

"I don't see how she can do that." Miss Weld's voice had gone thin, and Willelm looked at her sharply. He had not missed the tone of censure in her voice.

"I believe it is your brother inciting her to do so." Willelm knew his own voice was frosty, as much in defence of his friend as the jealousy that sprang up again.

"I only mean that I don't know how she can not be afraid of falling," Miss Weld replied after a slight pause. He glanced at her, and whether the clarification was truthful or abashed he could not say.

"Juliana is not afraid of very many things," Willelm said, turning back. He watched Juliana hesitate, then laugh and shake her head. She used Anthony's hand to step down instead, and Willelm breathed out.

"We used to come here often when we were children, and I don't believe she's lost her climbing ability." A sudden laugh shook Willelm, though he felt pained. "You shall have a chance to see her ride at my fox hunt, I believe. Nothing will stop her from following the hunt, even if she is required at times to avoid certain jumps. But she is the most intrepid horsewoman I know."

"She sounds remarkable indeed. I pride myself on my horsemanship, but I cannot boast about having followed a fox hunt.

My father would never permit it." Miss Weld moved forward toward the open tower, seemingly happy to keep Willelm at her side.

He glanced at her, and it dawned on him how unusual it was that she should favor a man like him with her conversation. He highly doubted she would have done so in London. Perhaps it was because there were not a great deal of other eligible suitors about. "I suppose Mr. Issot would have opposed it if he thought it would do any good. But he has a generous nature, and perhaps he thinks it would be unfair to ask her to curb something that brings her so much enjoyment."

Miss Weld stopped and turned to him. "Had you a daughter, would you prevent her from doing such a thing?"

Willelm met her gaze as he gave her question some serious thought. Juliana's laugh floated by, and he lifted his eyes in time to catch her gaze. He couldn't read the fleeting expression but thought that perhaps she did not quite like how much attention he was giving to Miss Weld. Or perhaps that was wishful thinking on his part.

"Were I a father, I suppose I would attempt to do so, but it would depend on who the girl was. If I had a daughter like Juliana, I don't believe I would have the heart to keep her tightly bound."

"And yet it is the father's role to see to the safety and security of his daughter, is it not?" Miss Weld continued to meet his gaze, curious and searching.

Willelm had not expected to have such a forthright conversation with Miss Weld, and it improved his opinion of her. "I believe the father's role is to see to the safety of his children, but he must balance that with their natural strengths and desires. One cannot be too forceful in one's parenting." Willelm was thinking of his own father—a man who had never taken Willelm's desires or inclinations into account.

Miss Weld released him from her gaze but did not remove

her hand from his arm. "My father would not have agreed, but I understand your point. What is on the other side of the arches?"

Willelm took that as a sign that she was content to continue walking with him. And he was not displeased to find that there was more to her than what he had first assumed. "We must see this tower first, and then we may go to the cloisters on the other side."

Juliana was now separated from the gentlemen and had stopped as though to wait for him. However, he could not very well leave Miss Weld or change his course after stating his intentions. He acknowledged Juliana with a friendly nod, then turned into the square tower whose tall sides nearly blocked the light. After all, he had promised himself he would keep his focus on his companion—and *not* on the flashing smile of his child-hood friend.

Sharow Estate, Friday 15<sup>th</sup> December, 1815

Dear Tempie,

It has been nearly a month since I last wrote, for it has been quite frenzied. I was delighted to receive your letter in return, agreeing to my friendly wager. I fear you have already gained a lead on me, because I have merely assembled my guests in place, including your darling great-niece and -nephew, who have greatly added to the enjoyment of our house party. However, from what I've seen of my two protégés, they have not sought each other out for enough *tête-à-têtes* to suit my taste. They remain practically strangers! At this rate, you shall win with no trouble at all.

Willelm does not express his feelings very easily, and Juliana is high-spirited and likely cannot appreciate the value of someone whose nature is so different from her own. They have had a few moments together in the week they've been here, and when they've gone riding, it was always in a group. There is nothing close to the sparks I had hoped to see. Tell me you are finding it as hard as I am so that I may not despair of winning. However, although I do not throw my cap after lost causes, I am far from predicting my intended match to be a failure. I still have a few tricks up my sleeve, and if the fox hunt is not something to bring them together, then I may indeed have to concede defeat.

Do let me know how you are going on. I am enclosing with this note an unfinished letter I had written with the Christmas festivities and improvements on the west wing of our house that you had asked about. I shall leave you with this note and send it off without further delay so that you may be encouraged to respond to me in return. After all, the Christmas season has hardly begun, and there has not been time for it to work its magic. There is something about the soft light of candles over dinner, the smell of greenery, and the sounds of carols filling the air that do something to a hardened heart. May its gentle bewitchment fall on Willelm and Juliana.

Yours most affectionately,
    Euota

# CHAPTER 7

Juliana walked in the main hall, where the sounds of servants speaking Yorkshire greeted her ears and the scents of slow-roasted game with garlic and thyme floated through the ground floor, teasing her nostrils. She entered the library, which was empty at present, and walked over to the window. A brown-and-green pheasant perched on the wooden gate topped with snow before making a short, abrupt descent to a patch of grass. The view beyond, with the expansive meadow and barren trees in the distance, touched her with its pleasing stillness. London so rarely stopped in this way.

The outdoors called to her, and she decided to greet Sunbeam, the favorite mare of her godmother's, who was hers to ride whenever she visited. At her feet, Hazel looked up at Juliana expectantly with something very much like a grin.

"Well, Hazel? Shall we go out?" The terrier barked, then scampered toward the door, and Juliana followed. "Don't be so hasty. I must fetch my cloak first. *I* have no fur."

Juliana exited the house just as tiny white flakes began to fall. Her boots thumped on the frozen path as Hazel ran off, leaving behind a zigzagged trail of footprints in the meadow. Juliana's breath came out in puffs as she walked toward the stable.

After one week in Yorkshire, she had to admit the house party was more pleasurable than she had expected. Of the other three women, she was beginning to develop a new appreciation for Emma, whose conversation was uncomplicated and pleasant. True, she was not entertaining, but she was dependable and sweet and did not require one to be always on one's guard as in London. Juliana liked Margery well enough and found her practical frankness refreshing. She had been surprised to learn that Margery was betrothed to a gentleman in York, and that the wedding was to occur in March.

As for Clarissa Weld, Juliana decided to withhold judgement. Knowing that she moved in the first circles in London, Juliana could not help but respect her. But Clarissa did not come across as particularly warm—nor was Juliana certain just how sincere she was. As Clarissa had spent considerable time talking to Willelm, she found her doubts on the subject troubling. Willelm did not deserve to be hurt.

The gentlemen were easier to categorize. Juliana easily dismissed Matthew from her consideration as a possible suitor. It was not that she wished to be heartless, but as little as she relished his limited conversation, he seemed disinclined to expand it. She did not feel guilty for seeking amusement elsewhere.

Thomas was as fun as she remembered him, but he had a distracted air about him that seemed entirely new. *Or* he had changed a great deal since they were children. He laughed and teased her at one moment, but then he appeared to withdraw the next—brooding, almost. Before his arrival, she had entertained the notion of him as a promising match. Now she knew she could not attach herself to someone whose moods were so changeable.

As for Anthony Weld…in many ways, he was just what she

was looking for in a potential suitor. He had a London house—large, from what she had heard—and spent his days in precisely the manner she liked, except for his tendency to keep to his bed until noon. Why, that was the day wasted! There were horses to ride and dogs to walk and people to see. Perhaps he could be broken of that bad habit...

Juliana trudged toward the stable, caught up in how such a thing might be achieved—a train of thought her sister would describe as calculating. However, how could a young lady help but calculate if she wished to make a good match? Juliana was certainly not willing to leave it all up to fate. Pulling Anthony away from the bustle of London gave her a greater opportunity for getting to know him and, if interested, attracting his notice. Why *had* the Welds come to Yorkshire, come to think of it? She had yet to ask her godmother, but she must do so.

Juliana had had plenty of occasions to speak to Willelm, but they were always in the company of others, and their lines of conversation adhered to the most benign subject matters. She had not missed his special attention to Clarissa Weld during the visit to Fountains Abbey, nor his continued attention in the days afterwards. At times, Juliana would feel his regard on her, and it sparked a warmth in her heart. She knew he had not wholly dismissed her as someone of importance in his life, even if he no longer gave her his undivided attention. That last fact bothered her more than she would care to admit.

She entered the stable and went directly over to the Thoroughbred mare, who lifted her ears at the sight of Juliana. "It's me, you gorgeous creature. Have you missed me? No, there is no point in sniffing about. I have utterly failed you by forgetting to bring an apple. I promise I will bring two next time."

While Juliana stroked Sunbeam's neck, Hazel sniffed around the straw and began digging in a fury in one darkened corner.

"What did you find there, Hazel? Do you intend to rid the stable of all its nasty rodents?"

"Juliana."

Willelm's voice brought her whirling about, and a flash of self-consciousness engulfed her at their first meeting without an audience. He moved toward her until he came abreast, and there was the slightest pause before he spoke. "I was just coming to ride. Is that what you were doing?"

"No, I'm not dressed for it. I just wished to see Sunbeam." She gave one final pat to her horse. "But I'll wait while you saddle Valour, if you wish." Juliana knew he rarely asked for help from the groom unless he was pressed for time. This was the sort of detail he liked to see to himself.

"Very well. If you have time, come along!" He walked forward to the stall where his horse was kept, and she followed. She wanted to ask him how his shoulders and arms had gotten so broad his jacket barely fit him anymore but felt strangely shy.

Juliana stood at the edge of the stall while Willelm went over and pulled the harness off the hook on the side of the stable and brought it over. The groom was not in view, and there were sounds of the stable hands turning straw in the stalls on the far end. A comfortable silence fell between them as Willelm harnessed his Thoroughbred, then brought the saddle over from the peg and placed it over the blanket on the horse's back.

A question had been humming in Juliana's mind as she watched these proceedings, which she was not sure was wise to voice. She shouldn't ask, she supposed, but the more she hesitated, the more the desire to know bubbled up inside of her until she couldn't contain it anymore. With her eyes on the horse in front of her, her hands patting its flank, she asked, "Do you plan to marry?"

She felt his surprise at her question by the abrupt turn he made at her side. "Why do you ask me that?"

That was the one thing she had hoped he wouldn't ask her, because she had no idea why. The question had come out of her mouth before she could rein it in.

She bit her lip, still refusing to meet his gaze. "We're old friends, so I suppose I took the liberty. I hoped the question would not be taken amiss." She drew a breath. "Also, you've always struck me as someone who *should* marry and have many children. You need a family life far different from the one you had growing up."

He cleared his throat. And from the corner of her eye, she saw him look down at the ground. His stallion nudged him when Willelm's silence grew weighted.

"Oh, Juliana." Her name came out of his lips like a sigh, and it wrung her heart. It was as though he wanted something from her, but she suspected it was more than she could give. "You know that I went to London with the intention of courting you."

She swiveled in an instant to meet his gaze. The significance of his words came rushing back at her and had her turning away again when a blush mounted to her cheeks. She supposed she *had* known deep down—a woman could always tell these things. But what could she have done when she had not felt the same way? There were times when she thought that maybe she could, but those times were fleeting.

"I did not know it. I am not sure it is what I would've wanted."

The chuckle that escaped him surprised her, and she glanced up at him. "Don't I know it," he replied. "You told me you did not come to London to dance with your playmates."

The conversation should have been awkward—and it was to some extent—but it also felt comfortable, and for some reason she could not identify, she did not wish to end it.

"I suppose that was rather harsh of me. I apologize. But it was true at the time. I was enjoying myself too much to want anything to do with Yorkshire."

"And now?" His voice was curious and held a thread of hope.

Juliana stopped stroking the horse's side and turned to him.

"I have mixed feelings, if I am to be perfectly honest. On one hand, I do not wish to marry you. We are friends, and your life is in Yorkshire and mine is in London. But...on the other hand, I don't like watching you talk with any of the other young ladies because you are *my* friend. And I miss our conversation when you are giving it to someone else." She stopped suddenly and laughed. "It is probably most inappropriate for me to talk to you this way. How my mother would scold."

Willelm folded his arms, increasing the tension in his coat, and his lips turned up in a slight smile that held a hint of sadness. "This is exactly the kind of conversation I can expect from you," he said. "It is perfectly frank and ingenuous, and I've never met another person with whom I can talk like this. On the other hand, your words make it clear that I need to look elsewhere if I want to settle down. And that must naturally mean that our friendship has to have some distance."

She furrowed her brows, hating the thought. "But why? If we're friends, nothing should come between us—not even a spouse."

Willelm reached out and laid a hand on Juliana's shoulder. With a slight shake of his hand, he could nudge her like a big brother. With a slight shift to the nape of her neck, he could caress her face like a lover. That last thought barreled through Juliana's mind so that she almost missed his words. "But I want my greatest friendship to be with my spouse. There will be no one else dearer to me than her."

Juliana fought an inexplicable desire to weep. Everything he said made sense, but it seemed unfair. Why couldn't she have the glamor and excitement of London and the dashing husband who would give that to her, alongside the comfort and friendship of Willelm?

The Saviles' groom came into the stable and saw that the saddle on Willelm's horse was unbuckled. "Nah then. If tha's fixin' t'ride, I can fettle her."

Willelm glanced at Juliana, then stepped out of the stall to make way for the groom, handing him the reins. "Thank you, John. I will just walk Miss Issot to the house and return to ride."

They left the stable, and Willelm held out his arm for Juliana to slip her hand around it. They strolled across the snowy landscape in a silence that should have been more uncomfortable than it was after the conversation they had just shared.

Juliana had taken hold of her emotions and no longer felt like crying. What he had said made perfect sense. Of course when she married, her husband would also be the most important person in her life—even more so than an old friend like Willelm. The problem was that she had never encompassed the idea of friendship when considering a spouse. She had easily been able to dismiss Willelm's importance in her life in London, where she had more exciting things to look forward to. Now that she was home again, and in Willelm's presence, the old pull of his friendship called to her and tempted her, its cornerstone rich with comfort. That made her nothing better than a fair-weather friend, which was a lowering thought.

She assumed a cheerful voice when she said, "You said you would have to look elsewhere. Do you have someone in mind?"

He glanced at her, and in the late morning light, she saw the rare sign of stubble on his chin that showed he had not yet shaved. She studied his aquiline nose and the firm lips he turned her way. The warm winter light turned his eyes the color of the sea, and he fixed those eyes on her for a long moment before speaking. She saw all this, and a possessiveness rose up in her. Willelm was *her* friend, and he could not possibly have this kind of connection with another woman, even if she was his spouse.

"I believe I might begin pursuing Miss Weld while she is here, with an aim to matrimony." He kept his eyes on Juliana until the moment seemed to grow tense, then looked away.

His words pierced the bubble of loyalty and possessiveness that had enveloped her, and Juliana turned her face forward, loosening her grasp on his arm. "I see." She quirked her lips upward in an attempt at nonchalance.

"I do not believe she is indifferent to me," he went on, and Juliana was conscious of an overpowering desire to run. It took everything in her to continue putting one foot in front of the other at a steady pace. "She seeks my company when we are in the same room." He paused and looked at Juliana rather anxiously. "Would you not say?"

Called upon to answer, Juliana forced the smile. "I…I have not noticed, but I daresay I shall pay attention now."

"Do," Willelm replied. "And let me know if you think I stand a chance with her." He looked up at the bare branches of the tree just bordering the path, then at the house they were nearing rapidly.

"She rather rules London society," Juliana said after a brief pause. "I plan to ask my godmother whatever brought the Welds here for a visit."

"Oh, that I can tell you for myself. Miss Weld said she and Anthony wished to rusticate for the Season, but as their country holding is being used by their older brother for a hunting party they had no desire to attend, they were happy when Mrs. Savile extended the invitation. She is bosom friends, apparently, with the Welds' great-aunt."

"Ah," Juliana replied lightly. "Well, we are certainly fortunate they have come to liven our holiday."

"We are indeed. They have brought just that London spirit you might otherwise have missed in your month-long stay here."

Juliana found that difficult to answer, and as they had reached the front entrance, she called out to Hazel, who had begun to explore the meadow. Hazel came trotting at the sound of her voice, and Juliana reached down to pick her up. She hesitated when she saw the muddy paws. Her dress had just been cleaned, and she had no wish to put Betty to unnecessary trouble.

"Well, I shall leave you, then," Willelm said. He smiled, his eyes searching hers.

She couldn't meet his gaze and bent down again to pet Hazel, saying with forced cheerfulness, "Go have a good gallop. I shall see you this afternoon."

After a second's pause, Willelm turned to walk back to the stable, and she stood again to watch him go. How was it that she had not noticed what a fine physique he had? Hazel whimpered at her feet, and Juliana looked down.

"Yes, of course. You must be frozen. Let us go inside." She walked up the steps, and the footman opened the door from the inside. He must have been watching for her. Juliana nodded to him, wondering if it always felt so sad when a close friendship grew distant.

# CHAPTER 8

Willelm had been sincere in his intention to pursue Miss Weld, and his reason for telling Juliana had been to relieve her mind—to let her know that he was freeing her to seek her own path. If pursuing Juliana had taught him anything, it was that he needed to be a bit more dashing in his courtship. Instead of being a hero she could aspire to, he had approached the suit more like an aged widower in need of an heir, where any healthy female might serve the purpose. It was time he applied himself properly to the art of wooing.

As for the practical matter of carrying out his suit with Miss Weld, he experienced a degree of reluctance that was not very promising. It might have been in part that he was beginning to suspect an attachment between Thomas and herself. That would need to be examined. But since he was a gentleman in need of a wife and Juliana did not wish to take on the role, he would have to begin somewhere.

At the next opportunity, he sought Miss Weld out with the innocent goal of endeavoring to know her better. He found her in the drawing room reading a book, while Juliana, Thomas, and Anthony entertained the younger children with a game of hunt the slipper, and Emma sat conversing with Matthew as she worked on her embroidery.

"May I sit?" At Miss Weld's nod, Willelm took the free place on the settee beside her and glanced at the riotous game before turning his gaze to the window. He wondered if she might care for a walk. "Have you been outside yet today?"

Miss Weld closed her book and lifted an eyebrow. "Are you joking? It is the coldest day yet since we have arrived."

"Cold? Why this is nothing," Willelm retorted. "There is only the lightest dusting of snow, and the winds have not yet begun to blow in earnest. This is quite mild weather for Yorkshire, I assure you."

"You frighten me," Miss Weld said. She caused her eyes to go round, but he could see the smile lurking there.

Willelm smiled in return and wondered how to proceed from here. How was he to gain her undivided attention with so much bustle? He caught the gaze of Juliana, who stood in the middle of the circle. She quickly turned back to young Ann Greenwood and handed her one of her slippers.

"Cobbler, cobbler, where's my shoe? Get it done by half past two." She clasped her hands over her eyes, to the amused shrieks of the children and Thomas's admonition not to peek. Anthony handed it to Mary Greenwood, who froze as Juliana's eyes snapped open. Margery distracted Juliana's attention by pretending to pass the shoe behind her back to Thomas.

"It's Margery," Juliana called out.

"Would you care to go for a walk?" Willelm asked, tempted to join the merry party but unwilling to lose his opportunity to know Miss Weld.

"I believe I have already maintained that I am unable to bear the Yorkshire climate, so I assume your invitation is for some-place indoors?" Miss Weld allowed her voice to dip up in a question, and he could see she was teasing.

In truth, his invitation had not been for the indoors. Willelm, who was not afraid of brisk weather, thought that a walk in the beautiful Yorkshire countryside might change Miss Weld's mind about the cold, but he kept all this to himself. "Why, certainly. There are many places we might walk indoors."

He stood and held out his arm for Miss Weld, who placed her hand in it. They turned toward the door just as Juliana ran over and tickled Mary to retrieve her shoe. Willelm forced himself to turn away.

The main hall and corridors were spacious, and it was possible to take a turn of air inside Sharow Hall without having to retrace their steps very often. "Let us go to the upstairs picture gallery," he proposed. "That is the largest place to walk."

"As you wish." Miss Weld followed him but without exhibiting any real enthusiasm. Her signs of humor seemed to have fled.

She appeared elusive, and Willelm wondered if he was a fool to pursue her. Then, he decided that it really mattered not one bit. He would talk to her as openly as he would have done to Juliana. Either she would like him or she would not.

"What was it like growing up in your household?" he asked as they climbed the steps to the second floor.

"Goodness," she exclaimed, meeting his gaze briefly before turning her face forward. She waited until they had reached the top of the stairs before completing her thought. "You are not a proponent of polite, indifferent conversation, are you?"

Willelm felt a pang of chagrin and the accompanying heat of embarrassment. He was once again reminded of his inability to carry on a conversation according to the rules of polite society. Juliana forgave him for that failing each time he erred so that he could almost forget he had it. "I thought I *was* carrying on a polite conversation. I had just hoped to go beyond commonplaces."

Miss Weld seemed to digest this as they moved forward. "Very well. My family is quite typical. My parents' marriage was arranged. And as they have widely differing interests, my father spends most of his time at his club, and my mother with her...friends."

By the way she paused before the word "friends," Willelm wondered if she was referring to her mother's paramours, but he did not dare ask. Miss Weld continued. "Anthony and I have one older brother, who is heir to the estate, and we are followed by two other siblings. My sister will be presented this spring, I hope, and my youngest brother is still at Eton."

Willelm ushered her forward into the corridor that led to the picture gallery. "So you see, that was not so very hard. In fact, you said little that was out of the ordinary of what one might hear in polite conversation." He smiled at her. "And now I know just a bit more about you."

"All was fit for Society's ears except for the fact that my parents have an arranged marriage without any visible shared sentiments. That was a divulgence indeed. It is not something I bandy about." Miss Weld stared ahead, her lips drawn primly, and he could see it had not been an easy admission.

"I thank you for your confidence. In return, I will give you one of my own. I have no immediate family remaining. I was attached to my mother, who died before I reached manhood. My father died a year and a half ago, and it was not so much a trial as a relief." Willelm forced one foot in front of the other, wondering if that was too tedious a confession for such a new acquaintance.

"I suppose it is in the usual way of things," she replied. "I seldom meet families of our sort that are overflowing with affection."

They had by now stepped into the broad room of the picture galleries, and Willelm knew the portraits well enough to be able to point out the names of some of the family members, though they were no relations of his. After he had done that, he turned his mind to how best to return to their conversation. He did not wish to waste this chance to establish whether or not they might suit. He only hoped he was not going about it with too heavy a hand. *Enough with acting the part of someone's grandfather. You are to be a dashing young blade,* he reminded himself bracingly.

"Do you not wish for something better?" he asked her. "Do you not hold out hope for a marriage that is based on love rather than convenience?"

"I do not think much of love at all, in truth." Miss Weld turned her face to him as though to measure his reaction to her disclosure. "I am not sure such a sentiment exists, so I don't hold my breath hoping for it."

Willelm allowed his lips to turn up politely, but he thought that this was a sad avowal indeed. He was far from being sure he could attach himself to a woman who would not hold her breath expecting love. But perhaps she had never experienced such a thing. Perhaps it was only waiting for him to come and court Miss Weld in order for her to experience it. He lifted his arm for her to place her hand on it and turned their steps toward the drawing room.

Before they had advanced very far, Miss Weld came to a stop. "Mr. Armitage, I am not being completely honest with you. There is more to disclose, but I am not in the habit of doing such a thing. However, something gives me the courage to try. We are in Yorkshire, far from London society, and…I think I might trust you."

"You most certainly may," he replied, holding her gaze and waiting for her disclosure. He hoped he would at last see more of who Miss Weld was than the face she showed to society.

"We are here in part because my brother has a hunting party at present in Kent, and Anthony and I did not wish to attend. But we have also come because our family has had increasing financial embarrassment due to my father's—and now older brother's—gambling habits. Our time in Yorkshire will be used to reflect upon what possibilities lie open before us now. That we will need to retrench is becoming increasingly clear; yet in our family, no one but Anthony and I seem willing to take such a drastic step. Anthony is acting as though nothing is amiss, but I assure you, he feels it deeply." Miss Weld looked down, her mouth pinched. "I am sure you must despise me, but I hope you will not betray my confidence."

"You have my word," Willelm said. His first thoughts flew to Juliana. Anthony could no longer be considered a suitor, but she would not know that, and he could not tell her, having given his pledge to secrecy. His next thought was for Miss Weld.

"I am very sorry for your trouble and am very far from despising you. It is my earnest wish that Anthony will find a solution that will accommodate you both." He paused, hesitating to express the suspicion that had been brewing. "Do you fear you are not a candidate for marriage because you might have little in the way of dowry? Forgive me for being so bold, but I…I could not help but notice that Mr. Sutcliffe appears to have some interest in your direction."

As soon as the words left his lips, Willelm wondered why he had just said something so bacon-brained. Here he was, walking with a woman with the intention of courting her—and pointing out another potential suitor while he did so. He would never find a wife this way.

Miss Weld fell silent as a maid hurried past them, carrying a basket of freshly laundered linens to the guest wing on the other side of the portrait gallery. Only when the maid was out of hearing did she answer Willelm.

"I have not had a good example to inspire me regarding marriage, and I also fear I am of too practical a mind to consider a love match. As for Mr. Sutcliffe, I doubt I am the best candidate for him. He might look higher than me. If he marries into our family, he will likely get hounded by my father and brother to pay off their debts, and I esteem him too much for that."

"I understand. Thank you for your disclosure." Willelm wondered if her feelings did indeed incline toward love, but she was unable to identify them as such. In some ways, she was not unlike Juliana in her refusal—or fear—to submit to deeper feelings. With Miss Weld, it seemed there was only one course of action to take, and he proposed it. "Perhaps we might be friends."

"Friends!" Miss Weld arched a brow, softening it with a smile. "I have few of those. I will happily accept your offer of friendship." She held out her hand, and he shook it.

"I may turn my mind to your problem, now and then," he said as they retraced their steps to the drawing room. "But I promise not to betray you."

"Thank you," she said, giving his arm a squeeze.

That was a promising gesture—a sign of affection from her that could potentially lead to something deeper, should things not work out with Thomas. It should have lifted his heart to know that she might yet prove to be a potential marital candidate. Instead, he simply felt...nothing.

# CHAPTER 9

After the game of hunt the slipper had begun to pall, the children begged for another. Juliana glanced at Thomas and Anthony, hesitating, but the children's nurse came to say that there was milk and cake waiting for them in the schoolroom.

Master George Taylor was perched on Nurse's hip, and Juliana tickled his belly until he giggled. She drew Ann and Mary into a hug and leaned down to kiss Fanny, saying, "We shall have a game of fox and geese before dinner, I promise you."

When the children left, Thomas threw himself down into a chair with an expression that did not invite conversation. She wondered what could be the matter. He had been playing gaily enough until Willelm had come into the room. In a way, Juliana could sympathize with the plummeting moods, although it was not when Willelm came into the room that her spirits seemed to dip. It was when he left it.

That thought was not worth pursuing, and she glanced at Anthony, who had gone over to the window and was staring through it. She came to his side and looked out as well. The view was clean and inviting, and its peaceful silence settled something in her heart. London had much to recommend it, but it lacked the beauty of Yorkshire.

The cold could be felt through the windowpanes, and Juliana hugged her arms to her chest to stay warm. "How do you find life in the country?"

Anthony seemed to consider her question and glanced behind him as if to see if there was anyone in hearing. "What if I tell you I find it a dead bore?" He sent her a teasing smile, as though they must certainly agree on this point.

Juliana returned a light smile, although his words left a bitter taste. It was one thing for her to criticize her home, but it was quite another for a guest to say such a thing. For the sake of peace, however, she would take it in the spirit of teasing. "I should say I do not blame you. But you have yet to sample the fox hunt here. That will give you excellent sport, I promise you."

Anthony raised one eyebrow. "How do you know, my dear? It is one thing to ride to the hounds and quite another to follow with the ladies on a leisurely carriage ride. How can you judge what is fine sport?"

Juliana looked at him in surprise as a laugh burst out of her. "Why, my dear sir, have you not heard? I follow the hunt."

"*You!*" Anthony snapped his brows together, and the news did not seem to afford him any pleasure. "I will never believe it."

Juliana shrugged, gratified that she would have a chance to impress him and irritated that he found the idea so impossible to consider. "You will be forced to believe it in two days' time when we set off together."

He gave a sound of incredulity. "We shall see, then."

"Juliana!"

She was not dismayed to be called away to her godmother's side and leave a conversation that brought little joy. She sat on the chair near Mrs. Savile and patted her legs for the bulldog to climb up, giving him a lift when he could not quite make it. She tucked a blanket under his jowls to protect her skirt and started to rub his neck. "Oh, you are a dear, aren't you?"

"Hazel looks to be happy," her godmother said as she set perfect stitches in what looked to be a pillowcase.

Juliana glanced over at the terrier, who had worn herself out, first by a romp in the snow, then by attempting to chase the slipper as they had played until it had become too easy to tell who possessed it. Juliana had sent her away, and the dog had lumbered over to the fire, where she had laid down and since remained. Her godmother's puppy, on the other hand, had been banished to another room during the game because he was making too much mischief, alternating his time between chasing Hazel and the slipper. He had not been content to nap by the fire.

"She is perfectly happy, and she won't be jealous at all, will you, Pom?" Juliana looked down at the large puppy on her lap, who panted in reply.

"Are you enjoying yourself, my dear girl?" her godmother asked her. "You do not regret missing out on the London festivities?"

Juliana prepared herself to fib but realized that no lie was necessary, as she was enjoying herself. She nodded. "But it is not just me who is missing out, ma'am. You are unaccustomed to celebrating Christmas in Yorkshire and are also missing London festivities."

Mrs. Savile set a stitch and seemed to weigh her answer. "I have long since ceased to stay in London for its allure. I spent my Christmases there because my friends and I had formed that habit. But we get old, and these habits must change, of course."

"I find change sad," Juliana replied, thinking of her conversation with Willelm—thinking of his pursuit of Clarissa.

"It need not always be," her godmother said. "For instance… when you fall in love and marry, that is change. But it is a happy one."

Juliana pursed her lips and did not answer right away. She did not exactly equate falling in love with marriage. She equated marriage, rather, with making smart decisions to ensure she would have the quality of life she sought. A life where she would reside wherever she pleased and attend those parties that were sure to be interesting. It was a dreary thought to settle down with the first gentleman who offered, when another might come along with a better offer, and she would have missed out.

"I suppose," she said at last. She knew her tone was not convincing.

A smile lit Mrs. Savile's lips. "I never told you how I met Mr. Savile, did I?"

Juliana glanced at her with interest. Despite their advanced age, anyone with eyes could see how well her godmother and Mr. Savile suited. "I don't believe so, ma'am."

Her godmother sighed as she pulled a thread taut. "I was eager to leave behind the wilds of Yorkshire. I imagine we share that trait, considering you have not been back to visit since you made your debut. I had my eye on a London beau and thought that just about anyone would do as long as I could finally mingle with a larger society than the twenty or so families that lived near Leeds."

Juliana had ceased petting Pom, who laid his head on his paws.

"All I can say is that my plan was thwarted by my own clumsiness. I had on one of those large skirts that were fashionable at the time, and it got caught on the edge of the table as I walked by. It pulled me back sharply, and I fell *right* into the arms of Mr. Savile." She shook her head at the memory, chuckling softly. "He caught me neatly and, after only the slightest pause, said, 'If you insist, madam. Then by all means. I am your slave.' This he said in such a droll manner as one born to society that I fell for him immediately. Imagine my dismay when I learned he was from Ripon, no less!"

Juliana laughed, picturing the scene with perfect clarity. But the story gave her much to think about. She had not realized how similar she was to her godmother; yet Mrs. Savile seemed content with her life that would likely end with her residing permanently in Yorkshire. Hazel began to stir near the fire, and Juliana gave one final pet before letting Pom down. "Well, ma'am. It seems God had a decided hand in your fate."

Her godmother met her gaze with twinkling eyes. "He always does."

THE NIGHT before the fox hunt, Willelm invited those who were to ride in it to spend the night in Lawrence House. The hunt would begin early, and it was easier to have everyone in place. In the past, Matthew Clark had been appointed whipper-in, even for Willelm's father. Today, he would take on the role of huntsman. Willelm would be field master, but he wanted someone to take over whom he could trust, should the need arrive. Matthew had not much in the way of conversation, but he was an excellent horseman, and he knew the land.

Mrs. Clark agreed to join her husband at Lawrence House for the night to play duenna for Juliana, who would participate in the hunt. Mrs. Clark would follow the hunt by carriage with the other ladies, but as her husband and son both rode, she understood how important it was to Juliana and did not wish for her to be deprived. The rest of the party would remain at Sharow Hall and would follow the next day by carriage.

"Breakfast is at seven tomorrow morning," Willelm announced as their smaller party assembled after dinner in his drawing room. "No four o'clock starts for us, as we will follow only one fox and allow that to be sport enough for us. My gamekeeper will draw out the scent early enough for us, and I am confident that we will have an excellent hunt."

The guests did not tarry, what with the early start announced for the next day, and Willelm went over to Juliana's side as she handed her teacup to a servant. He waited until she turned his way.

"I cannot tell you how good it is to follow the hunt with you again, Jules. It is one of my favorite memories of our youth."

Her eyes were fixed on him with such a clear, interested gaze that the old flame of hope and longing rose up in him again. He tamped it down.

"I still remember the first time you insisted upon coming. I thought you were mad, but you kept up with the hunt, and you astonished the entire party—even me, who was already aware of your skill. I have to say that the annual hunts have had something missing in the years since you left."

Juliana smiled at him warmly. "I confess that my mother's reminder of the hunts to be had in Yorkshire weighed heavily in my decision to come. I would have come just for my godmother, but I almost could have come just for the hunt."

*But you would not have come just for me.* Willelm pushed down the errant thought that would do no good by being voiced. "So we are of the same mind, then, on the joy of the hunt," he said instead.

She looked at him with an air of surprise. "We are often of the same mind, Will."

Willelm did not find it easy to fall asleep that night.

The next morning, the servants brought out the standard fare for a hunting breakfast. Willelm watched Juliana eat it with relish, partaking liberally of the beef but not touching the eggs and brandy. He helped himself to both, breaking his roll in two and catching Juliana's sparkling eyes over her teacup. He could feel her excitement.

"You have not ridden Sunbeam these last two days," he observed. "She will be fresh."

"She will be perfect. If I cannot have my Dolly here, then

Sunbeam is the next best thing. Let me run up and get my hat, and I will be ready to set off."

Within the hour, the hunt party was assembled on horseback and ready to start. There were about fifteen of them, including the servants who were in charge of the hounds. By now, no one was surprised at Juliana's joining them, although Willelm had overheard Anthony express his skepticism to Thomas, who had quickly defended Juliana. *Wait until Anthony sees what an intrepid rider Juliana is.* He would eat his words.

Matthew approached Willelm to assure him all was in readiness. The dogs were sniffing the ground and darting back and forth, but waiting obediently for the charge. Willelm looked around and saw all eyes forward, then gave the signal. Matthew lifted the horn to his lips. He sounded it and gave a *halloa!* And they were off. It was a fine day—cold but with no wind. He led the gallop but did not push his advantage until Juliana pulled up beside him. He glanced over at her and caught the expression of pure pleasure on her face.

"Happy?" he called out.

"You know I am," she replied, and he heard her laugh. "Come on, Sunbeam. You will show these others how it's done."

They traveled through Studley Gardens at a gallop, following the hounds who streamed over the land in front of them. After going like this for some miles, the hounds slowed down and began sniffing about. Willelm allowed his horse to rest while Matthew rode over to the hounds. After a brief spell, the hounds were off again, leading them down into the park to a covert that was drawn blank. The field was allowed to rest their horses once again before the chase took off back through the gardens.

The dogs led them past Fountains Abbey to Spa Gyll. From there, the chase headed into the territory of Lord Darlington, who had given Willelm permission to hunt on his land. Juliana had kept up easily and, as if by mutual agreement, the two of them rode side by side, despite the fact that, as field master, Willelm should have been ahead of her. Two miles in, the hounds began to turn in circles, with the lead dog sniffing on the edges of a grove. She lifted her head, her ears perked back. They had lost the scent.

Matthew rounded up the dogs and led them to the east by circling back around. Willelm knew that his hunch that the fox had gone west was likely, since Matthew had the tendency to start the hounds in the opposite direction. Very soon, the dogs proved his instincts right and began sniffing, caught the scent, and gave tongue as they headed off toward the west. Willelm's horse leapt forward, following the hounds with Juliana right at his side. They were breathless, and neither spoke.

So far, there had not been any obstacle that she could not jump or circumvent by going a few yards out of the way. But now they were coming up to a larger wall that would be difficult for Juliana to clear on a side saddle, and Willelm called over his shoulder, "Head left, Jules, for the wall is broken in about two hundred yards, and it will be a much easier jump."

She obeyed without answering, turning her horse and speeding parallel to the wall. He knew she would find it and catch up to them without much trouble. Sunbeam was a remarkable animal and scarcely seemed winded.

Willelm rode on, dismissing Juliana from his mind for the moment, his focus on leading the rest of the hunt staff. Matthew had respectfully kept from riding in the lead, although he could have. But Willelm had allowed his partiality for Juliana to distract him from leading the hunt as he should, and it was time for him to lead now. He urged his horse into a gallop and pulled ahead of the party. In minutes, he caught from the corner of his eye the gleaming chestnut-colored neck of Juliana's mare. He was gratified—proud—to see how easily she had caught up.

In seconds, the mare even edged ahead of him—and the blood in Willelm's veins turned to ice. The saddle was empty.

# CHAPTER 10

J ust feet from the stone wall, Juliana lay supine on the icy ground, gasping for breath. The wall was a simple hurdle to clear, but she had not counted on the pheasant taking sudden flight from the ground on the other side of the wall, causing her horse to shy upon landing. After the leap, Sunbeam had changed course suddenly, and the next thing Juliana knew, she had parted ways with her saddle. Her horse had galloped off, relieving Juliana of the fear that Sunbeam had been injured.

Her assessment of the effects of the accident came in bits and starts, as did Juliana's attempt at breathing. A starling took flight from a thicket next to her, knocking snow onto her face. She blinked to clear her vision and focused on trying to draw air into her lungs, which didn't want to cooperate. After a few seconds of gasping, she was able to take one cautious, panting breath, then another. Juliana remained immobile as she regained the use of her lungs and began to appraise the damage.

There was pain in her left wrist and knee where she had landed, but neither place seemed sharp enough to indicate anything was broken. Her ribs ached, and it was still hard to take a full breath, so she didn't try. She lay there without attempting to move until the cold discomfort of being on the snowy ground outweighed the fear of movement.

Juliana sat up then and looked around, seeing neither her horse nor any signs of the hunt, which was no less than she expected. Slowly, she got to her feet, using her right hand and knee to support the weight, and shook the snow from her skirt. She tentatively flexed her left wrist, but the movement was uncomfortable, and she stopped.

*Well, Juliana. You can't stay here forever.* She tentatively put weight on her left foot, feeling the sharp ache of her knee and her ribs when she shifted her weight. Now she was fairly certain nothing was broken—she was just sorely bruised. Drawing a breath, she looked across the snowy field where the stone wall seemed to stretch for miles. They had crossed the carriages with the party that followed the hunt only once in their ride across the countryside. It would be necessary for her to seek to rejoin them, although she could not imagine how she was going to attempt such a thing at her creeping pace. Even if she had her horse, there was no way she would have been able to mount.

Juliana hobbled forward, stiffening her will. She had to find the small lane that led to a broader road where the carriages were likely to be. It was between here and where Willelm had jumped, and if she followed the wall, she would find it. After a few minutes at an excruciatingly slow pace, she heard the sound of hoofbeats racing toward her, and she turned with caution.

"Jules!" She heard the panic—and relief—in Willelm's voice. "You gave me such a fright. When I saw Sunbeam catching up to the rest of the herd without you, I could only think the worst."

She stopped and looked up at him, attempting a light expression through the pain. "You left the hunt for me. But you're field master!"

"Are you daft?" he exclaimed, a tiny break in his voice. "*Of course* I left the hunt for you, you ninny! Matthew will take over.

Are you hurt?" Willelm swung down from the saddle and led his horse over to her, reaching for her left hand.

She drew it back. "Sorry. My wrist…I don't believe anything is broken, but I am quite sore. I do not know how I will be able to ride, for I cannot pull myself into the saddle. And then—I have no horse."

"You will ride with me," Willelm said firmly, assessing her from head to toe. "Where else are you hurt?"

"My wrist and knee…my ribs. I think that is all."

Willelm's gaze left hers and followed across the countryside. "I'm not sure where the carriages are, but we ought to find them if we head west." He put his foot in the stirrup and swung his leg over the saddle, gesturing for her to approach. "Do you think if I put my hands under your arms it will hurt when I lift you up?"

Juliana smiled feebly. "I think it will hurt but much less than if I had to walk all the way to the carriage, so let us try."

Willelm shook his head. "You always were a great gun. I only remember you falling once before in all the years I've known you."

Juliana came over and turned gingerly in the way he indicated. "You must not think I announce it to you every time I fall."

Willelm lifted her onto the seat in front of him without squeezing her ribcage overly much, and she gritted her teeth at the pain she felt even with his light touch. He put one arm around her back, and, with his other hand, pulled her legs so that she was flush up against him. He gave a soft click of the reins, and the horse began to walk forward. "I know that must've hurt. I'm sorry. But we will go on at a walking pace and spare you further discomfort."

Suddenly, Juliana's heart filled with emotion at the tender way Willelm had rescued her. He had always been so attentive to her—he was like that with everyone—but she had rarely needed his help the way she did now. "Ah, Willelm, you're always saving a girl."

"Not always. Sometimes the girl saves me." She could hear the grin in his voice, but she wondered if he was talking about those months after his mother died. She had known instinctively then, despite her young age, that their friendship had fed him a steady diet of hope in those months and years after his loss.

Flakes began to fall, and there was only the sound of the soft hoofbeats in the snow walking at a steady rhythm. Juliana settled against his chest as lightly as she dared, breathing in the smell of lemon verbena essence that she associated with him, although that was not something she had realized until she was this close to him. His arms were solid and strong on either side of her, and his chin almost rested on the top of her head.

"Don't be afraid to lean against me," Willelm said, his breath coming out in a cloud above her head. "I do believe you are trying to be proper, but now is not the time for that. You must not strain yourself in any way until we can get you properly looked at. Lean against me," he insisted again.

She did as he bid, realizing only now how much she had been using her force to stay upright and what a relief it was to fully let go. As the horse led them onward at a sedate pace, they remained silent, and Juliana grew more and more conscious of the feel of his embrace. There were so many years of history, of laughter, and of shared interests that allowed her to fully trust him to hold her in such a way. She had never imagined, nor desired, to be this close to a man. If she thought about uniting herself with any man, it was to his possibilities for adventure, not for the comfort of his arms clasped around her.

But Willelm's arms held her in a firm embrace now, and a strange feeling grew in her belly, almost like the strength of a sudden flame on the wick of a new candle. Juliana felt tears prick at her eyes and her cheeks heat from the unusual emotion.

*I must be all about in my head*, she thought. The fall must have really shaken her to make her so weepy.

"Here's the road, and there are the carriage wheels. I believe if we follow this, we will catch them where they turn around." Willelm's voice was gruff, and she didn't answer right away, inexplicably unable to speak through the mood that had enveloped them. "Are you well?" he asked when the silence grew.

"I am well." The feelings bubbling up inside her had become uncomfortable, and she was glad that he had broken the spell. "Willelm, I am sorry I was not a better friend to you in London. You've always been a good friend to me."

The gait of the horse rocked them back and forth, and Willelm rested his chin on the top of her head. "True friends don't focus on momentary misunderstandings. That was London. We are now in Yorkshire, and it is Christmas. I don't believe we have fully allowed the magic of Christmas to lift our spirits, do you?"

Juliana grinned, though he could not see it, and she shook her head, feeling his chin as she did so. "Not nearly enough. But surely we must start thinking about it, for Christmas is nigh upon us. If I am well enough later, shall we sing carols as we did when we were younger?"

The sound of a carriage reached them from the distance, the wheels clattering over the frozen ruts on the road, and Juliana felt Willelm's arms around her, drawing her even closer. She didn't mind at all. In fact, in a curious way, it felt not close enough.

"Of course we must. Carols, decking the halls, kissing boughs—" he mused.

"What?" Juliana laughed.

"We shall do it all," Willelm said, ignoring her question and in a tone more brash than she had ever heard him use. She had no time to process what he might mean by the last, for that certainly had not been a part of their childhood Yorkshire Christmases. The first carriage was upon them, with the second one coming not far behind.

Emma pulled down the window from the forward-facing seat. "Oh dear! Juliana, you are hurt."

"Not terribly," Juliana said, struggling to sit upright on the horse and feeling the cold seep through her coat to her back. "However, I am certain I cannot ride and hope I might find a place in your carriage."

"Certainly," Clarissa replied, sitting across from Emma. "We have room in our carriage."

"Stay here," Willelm commanded, and he swung his leg over the horse's rear end, then stretched up his hands for her to fall into him. With a great deal of gentleness, he cradled her, with his arms supporting her back and legs, and lifted her slowly down. Then he carried her over to where the carriage waited.

The footman had descended to open the door, and she looked up at Willelm, suddenly shy to meet his gaze. "Thank you for coming to my rescue."

His look was serious. "Always." He turned his gaze to Miss Weld and smiled. "I am sure I can trust you all to bring her safely back to Sharow Hall. Miss Weld, will you see to it that Mrs. Savile sends for a doctor to see to her?"

Juliana glanced at Clarissa and was surprised to see something like a tender look pass between them—perplexed that he had addressed Clarissa rather than Emma, with whom he was more acquainted.

"You may," Clarissa said, shifting over to make room. "We will take good care of Juliana."

Willelm assisted Juliana into the carriage, where there was a tight space for her to sit, before tipping his hat to the ladies and climbing onto his saddle. He turned his horse and shouted, "*Gee up!*" Then he dashed off.

# CHAPTER 11

The riders were leading their horses at a walk in Willelm's direction by the time he caught up to the rest of the hunt staff and field. John Outhwaite rode with them, leading Sunbeam and he raised his hand to Willelm, who gave him a wave to let him know Juliana was in good hands. Thomas Sutcliffe spotted Willelm and steered his horse in his direction to ride alongside him.

"What happened to you?"

"Hunt is over, eh?" Willelm turned to follow the other riders and paced his horse with Thomas's. He had needed all the time it took to find the others in order to grapple with the sensation of holding Juliana in his arms—and to consider whether he had been as successful in removing her from his mind as he had tried to convince himself he was. "Juliana took a spill at the border of Spa Gyll. When her horse had caught up, I saw she had no rider, so I went after her."

"She all right?" Thomas glanced over as Matthew, who was riding with Anthony, caught sight of Willelm and waved.

"She's a bit banged up, but it appears there is nothing broken. At least, I should hope not. I deposited her in the carriage and asked Miss Weld to speak to Mrs. Savile about calling for the doctor."

They rode on without conversation, and Willelm listened to Matthew shout commands to call the hounds to him. After a short pause, Thomas wound the reins loosely in his hands, then unwound them.

"I've noticed you paying particular attention to Miss Weld since she arrived. I assume this is a new acquaintance of yours?"

"It is." Willelm did not wish to say anything more for fear he would inadvertently betray something of Miss Weld's situation.

"I warn you, she is not an easy one to pursue, should you have hopes of doing so." Thomas kept his eyes trained ahead, and his usually jovial mouth was set in frown lines. "If, for instance, you are hoping to win her fair hand or are hankering after her fortune, I advise you to proceed with caution, for you are not likely to meet with success in that area."

Willelm turned in his saddle to get a better look at Thomas. "It seems you have some interest in that direction as well, if I am not mistaken."

Thomas gave a bitter laugh. "I did once, but I was soon given to understand my suit was hopeless."

Willelm was curious and wished to know more, but he was too cautious to ask. The idea of seeing if he couldn't help Miss Weld and Thomas make a match of it took root in his mind. "Have you moved on, then? Given up all hope?"

"You would like that, wouldn't you? It would make the conquest easier for you." Thomas's frown had grown fierce, and other than a quick glance at Willelm, he refused to meet his gaze.

Willelm could make allowances for a man who'd been hurt in love, and he answered gently. "In the end, it is not up to me or you. It is the lady who decides who will suit her."

Thomas glanced over at the senior riders led by Mr. Savile. They had been lagging behind but now outpaced them. They were recounting the various stages of the hunt and analyzing what could have been done differently.

"I did love her, you know, and I want what's best for her. I am not saying I am so selfless as to appreciate seeing her be pursued by someone else. But I did love her. And it will be some time, I believe, before I can look elsewhere."

At this point, Willelm reflected on how to proceed. He could let Thomas know he was not seriously pursuing Miss Weld. She wanted only a practical match—even if he were not entirely sure that was true—and he had not yet rid himself of the desire to make Juliana his wife. Both facts made it clear Miss Weld was not for him. At least, she was not for him now, as things stood. However, he was not sure it would be the best thing for Thomas to think there was no competition for Miss Weld's heart, so he held his tongue.

"No matter what happens with Miss Weld, I am not your rival, Thomas. We don't know each other well, but we have a shared past. And I have no wish to hurt you or compete with you. I can only tell you that I am far from being sure Miss Weld is even entertaining my suit."

Thomas gave him a look of appreciation tinged with relief. It was the lightest Willelm had seen him since he had arrived in Sharow. "Nor do I wish for enemies." He stuck out his hand, and Willelm leaned over and shook it.

Whether it was from an excess of emotion or fatigue from the sedate pace, Thomas urged his horse into a trot, and Willelm was left to his own thoughts. Perhaps something might be made of Thomas and Miss Weld after all. He had compassion on her, for she did not appear to be a woman who could suffer the loss of fortune with any ease. And despite her declaration that she had no wish for a love match, perhaps Thomas's love would be enough to change her mind. He was not in need of her dowry; if only Thomas could convince her how little he regarded that, perhaps she might be made to care for him.

As for Willelm, though he had all but decided against pursuing Miss Weld, for some unknown reason he did not wish to make his intentions, or lack thereof, too obvious. He supposed at least part of his motivation was for Juliana's sake. As long as she did not fear him renewing his suit, she would be comfortable in his presence, and he could reclaim the easy friendship they had once had. He had missed it. Then, when she left for London, he could work on fully removing her from his heart once and for all. Only after that would he exert himself to find his own wife.

Willelm's thoughts drifted back to Juliana in his arms. She had fit perfectly there, just as he had known she would. She smelled delightfully like vanilla and oranges, and he wondered where she had procured her soap. London, most likely. When they rode, he had been able to hold her in much the way he longed to without giving her the wrong impression. After all, she had needed him. It had been a short ride of bliss.

---

THE DAY AFTER THE HUNT, Mrs. Savile gathered her guests in the drawing room to prepare baskets for St. Thomas's day. She had sent for a doctor to see Juliana as soon as the carriage had brought her home. The doctor had not been overly concerned and had said that nothing was broken; she would simply need to rest. Now, Juliana was seated on one of the settees with her legs up, and Willelm took a blanket from one of the servants and brought it to her.

"Here you go," he said with a wink as he lay it over her legs, then leaned down to tuck it around her waist. He could not resist the chance to reclaim some of the closeness they had shared.

"I'm not an invalid, *stoopid*," she said after a beat, teasing him with their childhood insult. But she had remained frozen while he performed the gesture.

He laughed and went to sit in the available seat beside Miss Weld. Only after he had bowed to Miss Weld and sat did he wonder if his choice of seats might have affected Juliana in some way. Perhaps he was still hoping for jealousy. But when he looked her way, Juliana's face was turned to her godmother, who called everyone to attention.

"Here are the dried goods that need to be wrapped up into something festive," Mrs. Savile said. "And you will find jars of jelly that still need ribbons on this table here. The salt pork is on the sideboard, and each basket should have a piece of that wrapped in cloth. We have baskets made up that need only a decorative ribbon, and we will need to sew pouches for the coins that we wish to give to the widows."

Willelm handed Miss Weld one of the baskets that was at his side and put another one in his lap. "Is this charity work something you have done with your family?"

Miss Weld set the basket at her feet before picking up her stitching. She was creating a simple purse to hold the coins, and there were green and gold embroidery threads laying on her lap. She smiled enigmatically. "My family is not so generous, I assure you."

"You seem to be enjoying it, though," he replied. He pointed to her lap. "Are those threads to embroider the purse?"

"They are. You must not spill my secret, however. Everyone knows I am much too superficial to enjoy such a thing as making charity baskets." She set her mouth in severe lines, but he could see hints of mockery in her eyes.

"Your secret is safe with me. This is something we've always done up here." Willelm glanced at Juliana, who now had her head turned in their direction. She quickly looked away. "It is essential to my own Christmas spirit to see joy on people's faces."

"I believe you must be right." Miss Weld licked the end of a strand before threading it through the needle. "And considering that I am not so very far from being in their position, I must appreciate the endeavor all the more."

Thomas had pulled a chair up to Juliana and was sitting with her while she wrapped white ribbons around the jars of jelly, using only one hand. Willelm watched them for a moment and was silent as he wound a silver ribbon around the handle of his basket.

After glancing around and assuring himself that he and Miss Weld were removed from the hearing of other guests, he turned to her. "I am about to ask you a very impertinent question. You may send me packing if you wish."

Miss Weld returned the glimmer of a smile. "If we are to be friends, then I suppose I can answer impertinent questions."

Willelm took a deep breath and met her gaze. "From what I can see, and from the things Thomas Sutcliffe has let fall, he still has feelings for you. Why do you not entertain his suit?"

"Mr. Armitage, you are an entirely different breed than London gentlemen," she murmured, her head bent over her work. "You do get right to the heart of the matter."

"I do," he said, in a tone perhaps too grim for what the situation warranted. He *was* of a different breed than London gentlemen, and he would not apologize for it. If certain young women could not appreciate it, then it was their loss, not his.

Miss Weld sewed in silence before responding in a low voice. "He spoke to me of his love, but I believe he is pursuing me under false pretenses. Mr. Sutcliffe knows me from London society, and he has proclaimed his undying attachment. But he does not know *me*. If he did, I do not believe he would offer me his hand in marriage."

The murmur of conversation in various spots throughout the room grew as the footmen brought in platters of tea and a variety of cakes and fruits.

"We must feed the hungry laborers," Mrs. Savile called out, and her announcement was met with laughter. There was a general bustle as people got to their feet and went over to select from the cakes. At her direction, a servant poured the tea for those who wished it.

"May I bring something to you?" Willelm nodded his head in the direction of the spread.

Miss Weld glanced over at the choice of sweets and replied, "A slice of lemon cake, if you please. And tea with one sugar."

Willelm brought her cake and tea the way she liked it. After selecting his own refreshments, he resumed his seat. "Why do you not take the risk of telling Thomas of your circumstances? Allow him to decide whether he is interested?"

Miss Weld took a dainty bite of cake and set her plate down on the table but did not pick up her embroidery. She waited until Thomas walked by them, carrying two slices of cake and handing one to Juliana.

"I do not believe that he will like me for who I am." She glanced at Willelm. "And I suppose I don't wish to find out."

Willelm put down the tea he had been drinking and picked up his basket again, grasping the ribbon that was dangling from the handle. "Well, as your friend, I can only advise you not to give up without knowing whether he is as inconstant as you think."

He leaned in until she looked at him, then raised his brows. "Sometimes people surprise you."

# CHAPTER 12

While Juliana sewed her pouch that would hold coins for the widows, she darted glances at Willelm and Clarissa, who had their heads bent next to one another in conversation. Even when Thomas came over to entertain her, she could not help but notice how Willelm got up to serve Clarissa when the servants brought in the tea and cakes. He seemed most attentive.

"You might become more accomplished at sewing now that you can't get around very easily. This should give you a chance to work at the skill," Thomas teased.

Juliana drew herself up with mock dignity. "I will have you know that if I wished to become proficient with the needle, I could do so. I simply prefer horses."

"Even when those horses throw you?" Thomas threw a ball of ribbon at her head, and she dodged, then winced at the pain it caused her ribs.

"Sunbeam did not do it on purpose. She's a good girl." Juliana drew her brows together. "If it was not from the pheasant frightening her, then I am sure it must have been I who rushed the wall."

"You shock me." Thomas said, picking the scissors up from her lap and playing with them. "You admit to lacking skill in riding."

Juliana lifted her shoulder and turned her face away. "I've changed my mind. I admit to nothing."

Thomas laughed. "I'm only teasing you. To own the truth, I have never met a woman who rode as well as you. How are you feeling today?"

Juliana tested her ribs by shifting a bit on her seat before answering. "I wish I might have injured my right wrist instead of my left so that I would have a good excuse not to sew. My ribs are still sore when I draw breath, but I seem to be able to walk with my hurt knee, even if it's a bit slower than usual."

"Do you plan to help decorate the rooms tomorrow? Anthony and I have talked about trying our hand at the saw."

Juliana glanced over at Anthony, who stood talking to Mr. Savile near the fireplace. It was one of the rare moments he was in conversation with someone other than Thomas, Clarissa, or her. He had not seemed to adjust to Yorkshire company as she had first thought he might.

"I could not miss the decorating. It is my favorite part of Christmas, although I do not relish taking all the greenery down and burning it before Twelfth Night."

Thomas reached down, took the end of a rope that lay near his feet, and began twisting it. He focused on tying bits of rope in bundles that would be used to attach the branches the next day. With a jerk of his chin, he indicated Willelm and Clarissa. "What do you think of those two making a match of it?"

Juliana looked down at her needlework, not knowing how to answer. It caught her by surprise how vehemently opposed she was to seeing Willelm pursue another woman, but she certainly had no right to ask him not to do so.

She chose her words carefully and replied in a low voice that would not carry. "It is time that Willelm married, but I am not so sure Clarissa is the one who best suits him." Feeling a sudden twinge of guilt for having said something so unkind, she added, "But then again, it is certainly not my concern. Of course, I have no say in who he should choose for his future wife."

Her statement was met with silence, and she looked at her companion. At last, he replied with a somber expression so unlike his usual cheerful self. "I, for one, think she would make him a terrible wife. Miss Weld is much too capricious, and he will have a hard time bringing her to bridle."

Juliana furrowed her brows. "I don't know. Willelm is kind, but you must not think that one can ride roughshod over him. He would never permit it."

Thomas responded with a disbelieving grunt, adding, "You, yourself, know what Miss Weld is like in society. *She* sets the tone. It is not she who is influenced. I believe that once she sets her sights on something, no matter how strong a man might be, he would not be able to naysay her."

Juliana glanced at the subjects of their discussion once more, then applied herself to her project. Thomas's words showed a certain amount of bitterness, and she could not figure out why he should feel so. She only knew that she could not agree with his assessment of Willelm. "We shall see."

Thomas excused himself and left the room, and Juliana listened to the quiet conversations around her. She had expected more from Thomas than this morose man he had become. What in the world had come over him to make him so jaded? Anthony moved over to sit with Margery and Emma, and she watched their lighter exchange. It was a shame that the Christmas spirit had not seemed to pervade the house and all its inhabitants.

Her thoughts drifted to those moments nestled in Willelm's arms as he rode with her. The ride had not been long enough. His embrace should have felt familiar, because Willelm was known to her. It was not like it was the first time he had caught her, or restrained her, or held her. But instead, the sensation had been entirely new. She had been aware of his arms and his closeness and his scent in a way she never had been before.

Juliana shook her head at the bizarre turn of her thoughts. They had no place in her friendship with Willelm. It was just an odd moment, borne of her vulnerability. It would surely pass.

THE NEXT DAY, Juliana's godmother forbade her from going to fetch the evergreens that would be used to decorate the halls, but she was not disappointed. She knew it would have been hard for her to trek very far, even if the carriage took her to where the woods were. Instead, she waited with impatience to see what would be in the baskets they brought, and she was already applying her mind to where the decorations could be placed.

Sounds of the party's arrival brought Juliana to the front entrance. Emma came in first, cheeks rosy, and laughing in a way that was becoming to her. Anthony came next, carrying a handful of pine branches. Matthew had a large basket of ivy in both hands, and the servants followed, bringing many more baskets and bundles besides.

"Let us focus on the front hall and the windows facing the park first," Mr. Savile said. "With what we have left, we can decorate the upper rooms. Juliana, I hope you were not too disappointed to have missed going out together for the decorations."

She let out a loud sigh but could not hold back her grin. "It was torture, I tell you. But I am glad I can assist with decorating the inside."

Willelm came in last, carrying another basket that looked to contain ivy and pine branches. He spotted Juliana and said, "For old time's sake, Juliana, come decorate the library with me."

She smiled at Willelm, happy that he had singled her out and happy that the object of his attention had not been Clarissa. "With pleasure!" She started to move forward but was checked by the pain and slowed her steps. Willelm came to her side and lifted his arm for her to lean on him, balancing his basket on the other side.

They entered the library, and he brought her over to the window before dropping her hand and setting his basket on the broad, white ledge in front of it. He put his hands on his hips and assessed her with narrowed eyes. "Perhaps I should have picked another partner. I don't know how effective you're going to be."

"You must be joking," she retorted, tossing her head. "You know I will be much better than any other partner you could pick—even injured—which is why you asked me."

They began unwinding the long strings of ivy and laying them across the sofa. Juliana glanced at him, wanting to talk, not about some trifling thing, but about something that mattered. She was unsure how to proceed. Willelm brought a cane-backed chair to the window and took a string of ivy before climbing up on it.

"How is your suit going with Miss Weld?" The question slipped out of Juliana's mouth before she could think the better of it.

Willelm paused in his movements of winding the ivy around the curtain rod. Without looking at her, he replied, "It is going precisely the way I wish."

That was a daunting answer. Juliana couldn't identify where the twinge of disappointment came from, but it occurred to her that if she were honest with herself, she had been hoping he would confess to not being interested in Clarissa at all. Or, perhaps he would tell her he had already proposed—though of course it was too soon for him to have done such a thing—and that Miss Weld had rejected him.

"That is good," she replied in a quiet voice. "I hope you will be very happy in marriage."

Willelm did not respond, but as he seemed particularly occupied at that instant in stretching to reach the farthest corner of the rod, she accepted that it was not the moment for him to do so.

Juliana brought the pine boughs over to the mantle and arranged them there to her satisfaction. Then she limped over to the side table and performed the same operation there.

"And how is your friendship developing with Anthony Weld? I haven't seen you spending as much time with him as you did when he first arrived."

Juliana heard the question when her face was turned away, and she focused her attention on the careful arrangement of the branches. Her response was a bit long in coming. "Oh. We are enjoying each other's company."

"How excellent." Willelm's reply was delivered in a dry tone, she thought.

Hers had been a vague answer, but she could not say anything more specific than that. For one thing, she had no idea of Anthony's interest in her. He seemed to be fickle. One minute he would pay her the most flattering attention, and the next minute he would bestow it upon Margery—even though she was engaged—or Emma. Or he would go off on his own and not talk to anyone. Contrary to when he had first arrived, she could not say he held any particular fascination for her. He was not as loyal and attentive as Willelm. And even though Anthony was a desirable catch by London standards, she was beginning to question the wisdom of seeking a husband who was so elusive, even if he did come with an elegant London residence. She found herself back to square one where her matrimonial prospects were concerned.

"What is this?" Willelm's statement pulled Juliana out of her thoughts. The accompanying laugh was loud, and it sounded forced to her ears. "Know what this is?" he asked, holding a sprig of green with fairy-looking leaves.

Juliana recognized it immediately. Mistletoe. "The famous kissing bough you spoke of when we were riding." She laughed, and it sounded no less forced.

Willelm walked across the room to where she was standing, and she felt her heart beat strangely as he approached. "You mean when *I* was riding, and you were being carried," he clarified.

"Very well. If you wish to say it like that." Juliana's face had heated up, and she wondered what he was doing waving that mistletoe in front of her. It was a dangerous piece of greenery.

He lifted one eyebrow and said, "I am determined that we shall have *all* the Christmas festivities to mark your Yorkshire Christmas." He raised the mistletoe in the space above their heads. "I would like my kiss, please."

His voice was teasing and his grin broad, but Juliana's heart pounded so loudly she could barely hear. She darted a step forward and kissed him on his cheek, then stepped back.

If he was disappointed, he didn't betray it. He brought his arm down, the mistletoe clasped between his fingers, still staring at her with a teasing grin. "When you marry, you will have to put mistletoe in each room of your London house to have a proper Christmas—and to make sure there will be plenty of kisses."

"I don't know about that, sir. I am not sure how much kissing will be done in my London home." Juliana stopped suddenly, realizing how naïve that statement sounded.

"You are not sure how much kissing will be done when you have a husband?" he asked incredulously.

Feeling highly uncomfortable and foolish, she put her hand on her hip and tried to look arch, but failed miserably. "I told you I plan on having a marriage of convenience. We both know how unlikely a match based on love is to happen." She grew more serious. "I want to marry for freedom, for life in London. I want to marry for excitement—not for love or any other foolish notion." *Certainly not for kisses.*

There were sounds of voices approaching in the corridor, but Willelm stepped directly in front of her, erasing the space between them. It was a proximity that would be inappropriate for anyone but him, being that he was such an old friend. Despite her trying to reason in this way to herself, he did not feel like an old friend in that instant.

He fixed his gaze on her, all signs of teasing gone. He remained still for a moment, though the voices and footsteps grew nearer, and it was not a comfortable position for either of them to be surprised in.

"You are mistaken, Jules, if you think that excitement can be reduced to having the right London address or being invited to the right parties." His voice was gruff, and he lifted a hand to cup the side of her face, his fingers sending shivers down her spine and straight into her feet.

"Excitement is being known." Willelm leaned forward as the voices approached the door to the library. Very slowly, he placed a kiss on her cheek, just next to her mouth where she knew her dimple to be. "And excitement is kisses—even ones forced by mistletoe."

He stepped back just as the door opened.

Sharow Estate, Friday 22nd December, 1815

Dear Tempie,

Your letter brought me joy in an otherwise overcast and busy day. I'm so glad you found your great-niece Florence a willing party to your noble schemes. But do you not think that Jessica's protests hide a deeper affection than she's willing to admit to? I must own, the thought had crossed my mind.

We had the most delightful day imaginable decorating the hall yesterday. This is not something I was able to enjoy in all those years we spent in London. Our rooms there are so greatly reduced. We put pine boughs on every surface of benches, tables, and mantles. And Emma and Clarissa crafted a large centerpiece made of greenery for the dining room table. Mr. Savile stuck a mistletoe up on the arch that separates the drawing room, but so far no one has purposefully walked under it with another. In fact, all the young folk seem to be avoiding it like the plague. The pudding is nearly ready, and I made sure to stir in my Christmas wish when Cook prepared it. I shall tell you if my wish comes true. We have plans to sing carols next to the fire on Christmas Eve. Then the Taylor and Greenwood children will serenade all the guests in their bedrooms, and everyone has been instructed to stay put so they might hear those charming little voices. It will truly be a magical Christmas.

There is only one fly in the ointment to mar my content-ment. I thought I was clever when I pulled Juliana aside to tell her of my own courtship with Raynald. Juliana and I are so alike, you see. My aim in sharing the story was to have her consider Willelm more seriously as a suitor and not let a preju-dice against Yorkshire close her heart to him. It seemed to have worked, for after he rescued her from a fall off her horse—

nothing serious, I assure you—they became as inseparable as they once were.

But then something has happened to set them at odds. Before the fall, there were moments when I could see their old friendship resurface, and other moments when I thought I saw jealousy. You must forgive me for being so calculating, but your great-niece and -nephew have been a particular blessing in helping my match along. Anthony and Juliana were spending time together, and Willelm and Clarissa also seemed to flock together. It is true there is always the risk that you might end up with two of my additions to *your* extended family, but I tend to have a good hunch about things, and I don't believe this will be the case. If the looks Juliana was sending Willelm were not precisely longing, they were not indifferent.

This development has therefore left me perplexed. Shortly after the decorating spree, Juliana took to her room. She claimed the effects of the fall were paining her and that she would rather rest at present. That would have been understandable if it had been just the one day, but even today she has not come to any of our meals and has had everything sent up to her. Willelm has been very quiet—too quiet, even for him.

I visited Juliana once, and she reassured me that she was perfectly fine and only needed to rest. Personally, I found her a bit listless. Willelm asked after her again today, and I could only repeat what she said. He had such a frown between his eyes that I know he was tempted to go up to her bedroom himself. I can only hope that this complication will not take on greater proportions and leave them more estranged.

We have just under a fortnight left, and although I am enjoying this matchmaking scheme, I believe it's making me more anxious than I would like. I could almost forfeit my winning just to see my dear goddaughter happily settled. Do tell me whether our wager is over and whether you have won. You seemed quite confident in your last letter. Since you will receive this just after Christmas, but before the New Year, let me not be behind in wishing you the very best of the season.

I remain, affectionately yours,
Euota Savile

# CHAPTER 13

Juliana was hiding. There was no other way to describe her burrowing in her room for the rest of the day and missing the late afternoon games. A knock sounded after dinner, and when she bid the person to enter, Mrs. Savile appeared, followed by Betty, who carried a tray laden with food.

"Ma'am, you should not be troubling yourself to walk about with your sore foot," Juliana cried out when she saw her godmother. She threw off her bedcovers and stood.

"I am no worse off than you, my dear. I had to come and see how you fared. Are you in great pain?" Mrs. Savile walked over to Juliana. She still leaned on her cane, but she seemed to be walking more easily.

"I am fine. You must not worry...I am only sore." Juliana did not elaborate. She *was* sore, but it was not her ribs or knee that troubled her.

"Well, climb back into bed, then. You shall eat something. I cannot send you back to your mother half-starved."

Juliana obeyed, and her godmother brought the covers up to her waist, then signaled for Betty to set the dinner tray on Juliana's lap. "You may leave us now," she instructed.

When the maid had left, Mrs. Savile sat on the side of the bed and studied Juliana, who made a show of picking up the fork. She could neither eat nor quite look at her godmother, who she feared would see right through her. There was an array of feelings coursing through her that Juliana would rather keep hidden, and they were entirely too close to the surface.

Never before had she experienced the battering in her chest she had felt when Willelm had stood within a hair's breadth of her before he had closed the distance and pressed a soft kiss to her cheek. The memory burned in her mind, and she came back to it again and again. Her heart had beat so loudly, she was afraid everyone could hear it when they entered the room.

"I am convinced I permitted you to leave your bed earlier than you should have," her godmother observed after watching Juliana in silence. "The decorating must have worn you out."

Juliana shrugged. "Only a very little. I would not have wanted to miss it, though."

It was not the decorating. The truth was, she could not leave her bed because she could not bear to face Willelm with all the novel feelings that had developed, nor could she bear to face anyone else. How mortifying that he had seemed entirely unaffected after he stepped away from her, but *she* had felt as though the ground were no longer solid. Rather, it had swayed up and down like broad ripples in the wake of a boat on a large pond. In the hours since he had pressed a kiss on her cheek, she had been consumed by sparks of joy and energy that might have inspired her to accomplish a million things, had they not been combined with a paralyzing lethargy.

Mrs. Savile patted her leg gently. "Well, I can see you are not in the mood for conversation, and I shall not weary you by forcing it. Take the time you need, and ring if you desire anything."

Juliana's lips trembled upwards at her godmother's kindness. "Thank you, ma'am. I will."

When Mrs. Savile left, Juliana managed to eat a couple of bites of her dinner before pushing the plate away. The food had no taste. How could she think about eating anything? She must be growing ill.

Her gaze fell on the slice of cheese that Matthew had acknowledged as a specialty from Swaledale sheep. Involuntary laughter broke out of her when she remembered Willelm's quiet teasing of Matthew at the dinner table that first night in Yorkshire. He was the perfect person to joke with, despite the serious bent to his nature. He rarely showed his humor to anyone else— it was as though this side was reserved especially for her. It was proof that she was his friend first before anyone else. For some reason, that reflection threatened to turn her laughter into tears.

Her thoughts flew immediately to the memory of riding with Willelm after the accident. As his stallion walked, Juliana had been rocked back and forth in the saddle, nestled in his arms. The recollection of those firm arms encircling her teased her vision more than once. It was an enticement for some longing she could not put her finger on.

The night of the hunt, when he had come to the drawing room to see how she fared before dinner, she had noticed for the first time how mistaken she had been in his appearance. Willelm was not stodgy; he was strong. In fact, his physical strength simply matched what she knew of his inner strength. And his face—so familiar as it had been all these years—had become appealing. There was a force to the attraction that pulled her to him, so that whenever she was in the same room with him, she longed to be at his side.

She picked up the napkin that was on her tray and twisted it absently, winding it around her fingers and remembering his arms around her as they rode, wishing he had pulled her close. And wishing that—instead of kissing her on the cheek as he had done in the library—he had turned her flush against him to kiss her on the mouth...

Juliana gave a sharp intake of breath, horrified. *Oh, good heavens!* She held her breath, shocked at the turn of her thoughts.

*I have accidentally fallen in love with my friend. Oh...oh...How long will it take to fix this?*

Surely falling in love—against all good intentions—could be rectified, could it not? She had not meant to do it, and anyone with good sense could see it was a most illogical thing to do. In fact, it was the stupidest thing ever!

She scolded herself. *Do not be ridiculous! It is time you took yourself in hand and stopped this nonsense. You know you do not wish to spend the rest of your life chained to Yorkshire. Besides, he's practically a brother—*

But Juliana was too honest to lie, especially to herself. He had never felt like a brother, even when the idea of aligning herself to him in any way had been the furthest thing from her wishes. He felt like a friend. A good, solid, dependable, sturdy friend, whose arms were rock solid and whose nearness caused her to lose all rational thought, whose lips...

*Stop it, now!*

But the train of thoughts would not stop. With a sense of frustration, Juliana took a minute to absorb the feelings she was experiencing and to accept them. Since they would not go away, she had little choice in the matter but to make sense of them. After the initial feelings of horror started to fade, she began to consider the prospect. Surely there could be nothing...*wrong* with being in love with Willelm, could there? He was a good man—the very best. He was a good match, and even her mother thought so. She enjoyed being with him.

True, it was a problem that he loved life in Yorkshire, but Yorkshire was not so very bad, was it? Juliana looked around the room and admitted to herself that she had not missed London once since she had arrived here. And it was not as if living in Yorkshire meant a life's sentence of rusticating. One could visit London, after all!

The potential consequences were a subject to think about presently. For the moment, Juliana could only contemplate this new development. Her heart beat dully, then she laughed suddenly, shaking her head. *I am clearly going mad.* She clutched her shawl to her chest and grinned, her eyes filled with tears. What an extraordinary revelation this was. She wanted to tell someone, but her closest friend was Willelm, and he was the last person to whom she could confide her change of heart. That would make it real.

She rang for Betty to come ready her for bed and clear her tray. The maid returned in moments and filled the silence by chattering about the preparations for the Christmas feast and the rest of the decorating that Juliana had missed. When Juliana's hair was braided and she had donned her nightshift, Betty bid her a good night, taking the tray of food with her.

Juliana was left to the peace of her room—the blessed peace—where she could digest this drastic change in sentiment. If only she could figure out how she was to face Willelm or anyone else the next day. No blinding clarity reached her that night, and she fell into a fitful sleep.

The next morning, Juliana was no closer to gaining the necessary courage to leave her room, and she ordered chocolate to be brought instead. The morning passed with her alternating between lying on her bed, lost in thought, and pacing back and forth in her room with nervous energy.

Shortly after noon, a knock came on the door, and Juliana startled and turned toward it. She wished it might be Willelm, foolish though that notion was. He would never visit her room. Such a thing would be highly improper.

"Come in," she called out, after sitting in the chair before the fire.

The door opened, and Margery, Emma, and Clarissa filed into her room. They stood in a semicircle around her chair, looking down at her, and it occurred to Juliana that it was the first time the women had come together without the men and without the older set. It was also the first time any of them had entered her personal domain. With their arrival came a certain degree of intimacy between them that hadn't been there before.

"Please sit," she said, indicating the sofa and footstool that were available. "I am sorry, Margery, that you are forced to sit on the footstool."

"Think nothing of it," Margery replied as she sat and tucked her legs behind her.

"We came to see if we might entertain you," Clarissa said after a moment's hesitation. "It must be lonely up here."

"Are you very hurt?" Emma asked.

"That is so kind of you. I…" Juliana paused, unsure of how to explain. There was a small part of her that longed to tell them about her new revelation. It had been so wholly consuming her mind, she was at a loss to imagine any other subject of conversation. But of course, she could do no such thing. The only one she might claim as a close enough acquaintance was Emma because of their history. However, they were cordial at most, and there was a barrier of differences between them.

"I thought you were improving," Margery said. "You ate dinner with us after the hunt and even helped decorate yesterday. Have your injuries worsened to make you keep to your bed now?"

Juliana furrowed her brows and searched for how to respond. She had already decided she could not tell these women she was hiding from a man she had recently discovered she was in love with. "I thought I was better, too, but I found that after decorating I needed some time to rest. Everything pains me more today, and I found it was wiser to stay put and truly rest."

"Willelm has been concerned about you," Emma said from her seat next to Clarissa. "He has seemed distracted."

"Has he?" Juliana brought her head around to look at Emma. Her heart lifted at the thought that perhaps his sentiments had not entirely gone away. Perhaps he had not been as unaffected as she had first thought.

"But never you fear," Clarissa said. "We are endeavoring to keep him fully occupied."

Her mood soured. She didn't want Clarissa to keep him occupied if it meant plenty of intimate conversations and chances for him to fall in love with her.

"Lovely." The word came out so bitter, Juliana attempted to infuse more warmth into her next question. "How are you doing so?"

Clarissa smiled and glanced at Margery. "Did you not hear us singing last night? Mrs. Savile has a harp in one of her rooms, and she had it brought in. It took a while for me to tune it, but I played the harp, and we sang a range of Christmas carols, did we not?" She turned to Emma and Margery.

"Willelm said he loves singing," Margery added. "One would not think it of him because of his reserve, but he sings with gusto. His hidden passion reminds me of Frederick. It is one of the things I love about him."

"Willelm does love singing." Juliana regretted that she had not been there to sing next to him. That was something they had always done together when they were younger, and he had such a rich, strong voice. Margery's comment about her betrothed penetrated her consciousness then. "Frederick is your betrothed. Is yours a love match, then?"

Margery's face lit up as she nodded. "I would not marry for anything else."

"How wonderful for you," Juliana replied softly. How odd that Margery, who was of such a practical nature, would marry for something as impractical as love. But now that Juliana had experienced its thrill for the first time, she could almost understand it.

"Tomorrow, we will gather in the drawing room for games and tea in the early afternoon." Margery leaned forward and laid her hand on Juliana's arm. "I hope you will be well enough to join us."

"I hope so too," Juliana said. She both longed and feared to see Willelm. What if he showed complete indifference toward her, and she were left to suffer from these feelings all alone? That would hurt beyond what she could bear. For the first time, she began to understand how her words in London must have wounded him.

She could not stay here forever. She needed to go and face Willelm, no matter what his reaction might be. Besides, she was not going to give up her entire Christmas holiday just because she was languishing in love. Tomorrow was Christmas Eve, and it was unthinkable that she spend it alone. Surely she was made of stronger stuff than that! No matter how complicated her feelings for Willelm had become, she would go and rejoin the house party. Tomorrow.

# CHAPTER 14

When Willelm did not see Juliana that night after he
kissed her on that tempting spot just next to her lips,
he was surprised but could invent any number of reasons why
she might not have joined the rest of the guests for dinner.
When she did not appear again the next day, he knew he had
made a grave error. He kept thinking and rethinking the events,
trying not to focus too much on how that kiss on her cheek had
affected him.

*What was I thinking, going and giving her a kiss like that?* He had
intended to step up on the seduction and stop wooing with all
the finesse of a grandfather, but instead he had been too eager.
The chaste kiss he had attempted had been anything but that.
He had barely been able to think straight when everyone had
poured into the room, and he'd had to pretend he had just
completed the decorating.

*She made it perfectly clear that she was not interested in anything
from me, and I resolved to give her all the space she needed. So what
must I do but go and try to seduce her? I am a complete idiot!*

Willelm wished he knew what she was thinking. If only he
could see her—read her expression and listen to what she had to

say. Had he frightened her? He didn't think so. Juliana was not somebody who was easily frightened. Had he disgusted her? He hoped not. He might not be her handsome ideal, but he certainly hoped that receiving one of his kisses had not filled her with disgust.

Was she trying to spare his feelings and hint him away? Out of every scenario that flitted through his mind, this one seemed to be the most logical.

He tried to fill his day by spending time with the other guests. He got up a game of billiards—a friendly competition with him and Thomas paired up against Matthew and Anthony. Anthony had not looked particularly happy to be paired with Matthew, who had little to add in the way of speech, but he soon discovered that Matthew was as good at billiards as he was a sportsman. They beat Thomas and Willelm two matches out of three.

Willelm had gone for walks with Margery, who appreciated the outdoors, where he listened to her tell him all about Frederick. He had played backgammon with Emma, but as it had been an easy victory, the game did not occupy his mind. And he had stood next to Miss Weld to sing as she sat playing harp. That had been a welcome relief from thinking about Juliana, even though he missed hearing her sing.

"You have a fine voice," Miss Weld had said to him during a pause in their singing, when the others were drinking punch and conversing in groups.

He looked down to where she was seated and focused his gaze on hers. "I must say the same about you—and you are able to do so while playing the harp. That you are accomplished does not surprise me in the least. But you sing with real feeling in your voice, and that is not something that can be taught."

Miss Weld looked down, and he detected faint spots of pink on her cheeks. "I enjoy singing. I suppose it is a way of expressing some deeper sentiment, although many would suspect I have none."

"I am not of that number," Willelm said, then glanced up when a movement caught his eye. It was Thomas at the fireplace, staring at them and wearing a scowl. Willelm was starting to lose all patience with him. The man gave up entirely too easily and brooded instead of fighting for Miss Weld's heart.

Willelm then remembered his own flight home from the London Season following the one remark Juliana had made and took himself to task. He must be more charitable—and maybe help the man out.

"Thomas, would you be able to bring Miss Weld a drink? I must...fetch something."

That had not at all been smooth, but Thomas wasted no time in coming over to bow before Miss Weld. His frown had disappeared. "I am happy to be of assistance, Miss Weld. What would you like to drink?"

Now that Willelm had stated his intentions to fetch something, he had no choice but to leave the room. He walked out with purpose, wondering where he was going to go. As he entered the corridor, Mrs. Savile was coming toward the drawing room at as brisk a pace as her cane allowed.

"Willelm. The very person I wished to see. Will you assist me in carrying in these prayer books? I thought we might read from them after we are done singing the Christmas carols. I cannot manage very easily with my cane." She turned and headed toward the door to the study.

"With pleasure," Willelm assured her and followed her in.

She made her way over to a drawer tucked in the central column of the massive bookshelf and showed him a small stack of identical books. "These," she said.

Willelm took the books in one hand and offered his arm so he might assist Mrs. Savile with the other. She put her hand on his arm, and they progressed at a steady rate back to the drawing room. He was glad he had something to do after all so his words had not been empty.

They neared the drawing room, and it dawned on him that he was missing out on an opportunity to do some sleuthing. "Why has Juliana not come down?"

"She said she had not realized how much her fall had taken its toll on her, and she thought it wise to take some time to rest." He could feel Mrs. Savile's piercing gaze from his side. "You wouldn't happen to know of any other reason she might have suddenly taken to her room? It happened so soon after you decorated the library together."

Willelm frowned to cover his embarrassment. "I have no idea. She seemed to be moving with little hindrance then."

"Ah, well." Mrs. Savile paused and allowed Willelm to drop her hand and open the door to the drawing room. "Eventually, she must come and join us. She cannot stay in her room and miss Christmas, after all."

"No," he replied, his heart dipping at the thought.

The next day was Christmas Eve, and Willelm was in the breakfast room early. He forced himself to eat, wondering if he would have a glimpse of Juliana today. He had certainly hoped she would not miss Christmas because of an ill-thought-out kiss, but he was starting to lose confidence. The other thing that troubled him was whether he should apologize to her. If it was needed, the smart thing to do would be not to waste any time. He wasn't sure he would get another chance once she left Yorkshire. He was willing—he just didn't know if an apology was warranted.

The door opened, and Juliana entered wearing a dress of a deep green color. She looked splendid, and his eyes drank in the sight of her.

"Good morning, Willelm," she said in a voice that seemed natural. But he read nothing from her expression since she quickly turned away to the sideboard to fill her plate.

"Good morning. We have all missed you. I hope you are properly mended," he said in quick succession. If he could just get a sense of the right way to approach her…

"I am feeling much more the thing. I still walk slowly and feel pain in my ribs, but I won't need to take to my bed any longer." Juliana's tone was cheerful, but she did not look him in the eyes when she came to sit at the table. She settled her gaze on the teapot in front of her and filled her cup.

Willelm was torn between concern and an urge to smile. He didn't *think* she was upset with him, but the fact that she couldn't look at him…did that mean she had been affected by his kiss? If she was, then not only had no harm been done, but it meant that perhaps there was hope. A foolish urge to grin overcame him, and he stood suddenly and turned to take another roll that he didn't need from the sideboard.

When he had his buoyed emotions fully in hand, he sat again. "You missed an excellent night of caroling. Miss Weld is most proficient on the harp."

"So I heard." Juliana's voice sounded flat, and Willelm wondered whether he should have brought up Miss Weld. After all, he hadn't told Juliana he had decided not to pursue her. Then again, he was far from being sure telling Juliana was the right thing to do. If he was wrong that she had been affected by his kiss, and she was still uninterested, he needed to give her the space to walk away. She must not think he was pining after her.

The silence grew, and he began to fear he was chewing too loudly. It was all he could hear. Where was the comfort he usually found in Juliana's presence? "This afternoon, we have games planned in the drawing room. Are you feeling well enough to join us?"

"I cannot miss today," she replied gravely. "It's Christmas Eve." The plate of food in front of her was largely untouched, and when she stopped speaking, she picked up her fork and pushed her eggs around on her plate.

"It *is* Christmas Eve. So you need to smile and stop looking so somber. Is this not why we are all gathered here?" Willelm smiled to add lightness to his words, and she met it with a brief one of her own, then looked away, blushing.

After a small pause, she cut her roll in two and spooned jam on one half. She picked up her knife and carefully spread the preserves. "Have you made progress in your suit with Clarissa Weld?"

Willelm swallowed his coffee wrong and coughed, covering his mouth as he thought how to answer. "I am embarking on a cautious suit and am waiting to learn which way her heart lies." Inspiration seized him, and he added, "A man cannot proceed in any suit unless he gets some encouragement from the woman. He cannot fabricate a courtship out of simple desire on his part. Do you not think it admirable when a woman can express how she feels about a man? It takes courage. And why should all the courage fall to the man?"

There! That ought to do the trick. If Juliana had any feelings for him, she now knew she needed to give him some sign. He would not push himself on her.

Miss Weld walked into the room at that moment and nodded to both before picking up her plate. "Good morning, Mr. Armitage. Good morning, Juliana."

Juliana stood. "Good morning, Clarissa. If you'll both excuse me—I must see what my godmother needs from me today."

"I am glad you are feeling better," Miss Weld replied as she took her seat across from Willelm.

The door opened again, and more of their party entered. Emma laid her hand on Juliana's arm and murmured something to her.

Anthony crowded in behind Emma and spotted Juliana. "Excellent. You are mended. We don't want to miss having you for our games this afternoon."

She turned briefly to murmur her thanks, then gave an encompassing nod and left.

Willelm had not been able to read any clues from her behavior. Juliana had been reserved, but it was not the reserve of London—the society reserve she wore like a cloak. This was the reserve of some emotion she refused to share, even with him.

He did not allow himself to dwell on it when he was in the eyes of company. He would try to seek her out later and see if she would reveal more. "Thomas, if you're looking for the bacon, Cook has promised to send another plate up shortly."

---

LATER THAT DAY, Willelm arrived early in the drawing room for the afternoon of games planned. It would be a chance for him to see Juliana at her most playful—to see if she had come out of her shell. He did not want to miss even a minute of time in her presence.

Mr. Savile was the only one there, and he was setting up for cards on the opposite end of the room. "Willelm, I've planned it so the older generation will be on this side of the room. That way, if you wish to play anything riotous, such as hoodman's blind, you won't have any older people breathing down your necks. Don't forget, I was young once." He winked.

Willelm chuckled. "I believe you still are, sir."

He didn't have to wait long for everyone to come into the room, and Juliana entered, talking to Emma. She glanced at him with a fleeting smile, then looked away. When would she again look at him properly?

Once everyone had assembled and was seated, Anthony stood to draw their attention. "I propose we play hot cockles!"

"No," Miss Weld protested, casting her gaze around. "That is much too lively. It is not seemly."

"What of it?" her brother retorted. "It's played in all the best drawing rooms, and what is Christmas for if not to have fun?"

Thomas stretched out his legs. "I say we play." He glanced quickly at Miss Weld, a hopeful expression on his face, then looked at Anthony, who was waiting for his sister's reply.

Miss Weld pinched her lips in disapproval, but as the suggestion was met with consent by everyone else, at last she said, "Very well, then."

"I'm so glad you agreed," Anthony replied in a tone that said he had known she would. "You may go first. I'll sit."

Miss Weld rolled her eyes but was so evidently teasing that Willelm had to laugh. He thought this side became her very well. She was not as stiff underneath as she liked to portray.

"I believe everyone knows the rules," Anthony said as he took a seat and motioned Miss Weld to kneel. "Someone has to come tap Clarissa on the shoulder while she has her head on my knees. That person will run away, and Clarissa will have to guess who it was. Easy enough."

"Don't forget the prize," Thomas murmured under his breath. But he did not seem to want anyone to hear.

Miss Weld knelt in front of her brother and buried her face in his knees. "This is undignified," she cried out, her voice muffled.

Thomas motioned to everyone to gather around, then he went up to Miss Weld, his hand hovering over her back before he tapped it lightly and darted back. Miss Weld got to her feet, her cheeks pink, as Thomas stumbled backward a pace. She looked at each person in the crowd, but her eyes came back to Thomas.

"Mr. Sutcliffe," she announced.

Everyone laughed, and Thomas put on a mock scowl. "How in the world did you know? I guess I shall be obliged to kiss you."

"What?" she retorted. "That is not the sort of game I am electing to play."

"Sorry, Clarry," Anthony said. "Hot cockles rules apply. You get kissed if you guess correctly."

"Had I known, I would never have guessed correctly," she retorted, but she turned her cheek upward.

Thomas came over and looked her straight in the eyes, then kissed her on the cheek. Willelm hoped he was having second thoughts about giving up his suit. He had abandoned it entirely too easily.

"Now, Clarissa, choose your man," Anthony ordered as he stood and joined the circle. The card players on the other end of the room made a noise as one of the teams took a trick.

Miss Weld looked around the circle, and her gaze settled on Willelm. A smiled played on her lips. "Mr. Armitage."

Willelm returned it. She seemed anxious to take the focus off her and Thomas as quickly as she could, and he could sympathize with her. He took the chair and said, "Thomas. Your turn. Who's it to be?"

Thomas pivoted to look at the crowd, then turned back. "I choose Juliana."

Willelm's heart leapt. It was just the person he would have chosen. He looked at Juliana, not daring to show any signs of pleasure that they were paired up for this. She looked at Willelm, then at Thomas, then crossed her arms.

"I am afraid I cannot get on my knees. They are still too pained."

"Of course," Willelm said, getting up quickly. "You sit here, and I will take your place."

"No, no," Anthony said. "You cannot switch places. That would be cheating. What you must do is to sit on a footstool. Come now." He went over to get an embroidered, cushioned stool and placed it in front of Willelm's chair. "Sit."

Willelm resumed his seat and waited for Juliana to sit at his feet on the small stool. She seemed reluctant to take her place for the game, and it occurred to him that it might hurt her to sit so low. He grabbed her hands. "Let me help you down."

She held his gaze, and he lowered her to the stool in front of him, not letting go of her hands even after she was in place. Once he realized what he was doing, he let go. She was sitting so close to him and in such a vulnerable position it made it hard for him to breathe. He refrained from clearing his throat out of nervousness and put his knees together and waited.

Juliana's face was bright red as she lowered her face onto his lap. Willelm kept his hands firmly at his sides. He longed to hug her or lift her face up and kiss her senseless. It was the strangest intimacy, and he felt the heat of her blush through the cloth of his pantaloons.

Margery held up her hand to claim the chance. She came over and swatted Juliana on the rump just above where she was seated.

"*Eh!*" Juliana's head darted up, and she swiveled around. Margery was laughing too hard not to be caught. "It was Margery. Please tell me I will not need to kiss her?" Juliana had raised an eyebrow, but she was smiling. She refused to look at Willelm.

# CHAPTER 15

Juliana could barely get through the game of hot cockles without feeling that she was going to die of mortification. It was not the first time she had buried her head in Willelm's lap, for they had often played the game as children for tickles instead of kisses. But never had she been so conscious of what she was doing. *Good heavens*—how was such a game fit for proper society? And yet it was played all over England.

Every one of the young people had their turn to swat or be swatted before they wore themselves out from laughing.

After the game had run its course, her godmother called Juliana over and invited her to sit beside her. "My dear, it is so good to see you well enough to mix with company again. All that silliness between you young people is just what I had hoped to see this Christmas. I had begun to fear you would be too unwell to attend the Christmas festivities."

"No, that would be unthinkable," Juliana replied, suffering a twinge of guilt for having absented herself for no other reason than being unable to come to terms with the novel feelings she was experiencing. "I've already missed the carols, but I'm doing much better and will not miss the lighting of the Yule log tonight—or our special Christmas Eve dinner."

"Good." Having received that assurance, Mrs. Savile sat back. "I've been thinking. Although you missed our night of caroling, I wonder if you would help train Ann, Mary, and little Fanny on their Christmas carols? It can be daunting for young ones to sing in front of the bedchambers. I'm sure your help would give them the confidence they need."

Juliana's heart lit at the idea; it was the perfect way to keep from torturing herself over Willelm. She beamed at her godmother. "You know how much I adore the tradition of children rousing the household with their sweet voices on Christmas morning. I would be happy to help them prepare."

Mrs. Savile glanced up as the footmen brought in tea and cakes. "Wonderful. I knew you would agree to it. I was thinking perhaps you might write out three or four carols so that Ann and Mary have the words? Fanny will just follow along."

Juliana nodded, searching her memory for the most appropriate carols. "I am sure they must be familiar with '*We Wish You a Merry Christmas*,' so that can be one of the four songs. I will write the words, though, in case they get nervous. Now I must think of three others."

Her godmother reached over and squeezed Juliana's hand. "Mrs. Greenwood told me they take their task very seriously. They will be delighted for you to come and instruct them. When you have had your tea, you will find the children in the playroom with their nurse."

Juliana glanced at the platters of heart cakes and gingerbread that were now on display next to a selection of china cups and saucers. "*Mmm*. Delicious. I will take tea in my room so that I do not waste a precious minute. I can write the carols at the same time."

Juliana selected her refreshments, then headed toward the door but was stopped short by the sound of Willelm's voice.

"Juliana, I thought you would be taking tea with us. Don't run to your room and hide there again."

She turned and started toward him, tempted to stay, until she noticed that the seat beside him had been taken by Clarissa Weld. "I'm not *hiding*," she replied, trying not to sound affronted. "I promise I will be back for the rest of our activities, but I must help the children with their morning carols."

"Well, be quick about coming back. Anthony has declared that we are all to go outdoors." Willelm grinned at her, then turned his attention to Clarissa. Juliana tried not to let her heart sink at his obvious interest in another woman. Still, she could not be sure all hope was lost. Had he not given her some distinct signs of encouragement? He must simply be acting the part of the gentleman, surely. A footman opened the door for her, and she swept through, plate and saucer in hand as she climbed the steps, wrestling with these thoughts.

In her room, Juliana sat in the chair facing the fire and placed her tea on the table next to her, grateful for the chance to be alone and settle her thoughts. She was swimming in a sea of feelings that left her out of her depth. She still felt a sense of wonder that at last she returned Willelm's regard. She basked in that happy realization until she remembered his regard was possibly no longer pointed in her direction.

How could she have dismissed him in London? How could she not have seen that he was the right one for her? And now he showed signs of having moved on to someone else, and she was left wading through these newfound emotions with no remedy. It seemed her only solution for not staring longingly after Willelm was simply not to look at him at all. But then she *thought* about him. In fact, she thought about little else.

*What if I simply told him how I felt?* Juliana drained the rest of her tea, her heart growing jittery at the thought of being honest about her feelings. She had never done such a thing. Perhaps it might please him. Perhaps he was only waiting for her to do so before rushing to her side. Did he not say he wanted a wife who possessed the capacity to express the deeper matters of her heart?

In the safety of her room, Juliana elaborated on this idea. She considered what it would be like to tell Willelm—her *friend*, who had already confessed having feelings for her—that she returned his regard. After minutes of wrestling within herself, she steeled her resolve and went over to the desk, where there was a quill and inkwell.

She breathed out. *First things first: Christmas carols for the children.* Putting to the side for the moment the idea of confessing her feelings to Willelm, she lifted out a piece of paper from the narrow desk drawer and set it in front of her.

She wrote down the words to *"We Wish You a Merry Christmas."* Next, she decided upon *"Joy to the World"* and *"The First Noel."* There was now a mix of cheerful and meaningful carols to awaken the household to the joys of Christmas morning.

*One more!* Juliana's heart began thumping again with her idea, but she focused on her task at hand. *"God Rest You Merry Gentlemen"* would be perfect for a fourth carol. It was a song she loved dearly. True, Clarissa had mentioned it was a favorite of hers as well, but she would not give in to jealousy.

> *God rest you, merry gentlemen,*
> *Let nothing you dismay.*

JULIANA BEGAN to write a verse of it on a fresh sheet of paper. When she came to the end of the first verse, it occurred to her that she didn't know the other ones by heart. Although she knew she could go and find her godmother to ask her, Juliana remained frozen in place. Her lip caught between her teeth, she began sketching a holly leaf, then berries, then a pine bough as the idea for a verse that had nothing to do with Christmas and everything to do with Willelm began to brew in her mind.

Seized by inspiration and a hammering of her heart, she wrote that verse out quickly, then paused. It was about their shared childhood and how she felt in his presence. She thought some more and added another verse, letting him know how much she regretted her quick rejection of him. Heart in her throat, she added one final verse declaring that she would wait for him in the library on Christmas morning should his feelings remain the same. Before she could lose courage and change her mind, she sprinkled the paper with sand and shook off the excess.

Now Willelm would know how she felt. If he wished to act upon the knowledge, he would come and find her. There was no surer sign she could give him than that.

Hands trembling, Juliana folded the paper in three and wrote Willelm's name on the outward fold. There would only be three Christmas carols for the general public and one carol for Willelm Armitage. Now all she had to do was to see if the girls could be relied upon to sing this for him and not say a word about it otherwise.

She hurried toward the schoolroom as quickly as her injuries would allow and reflected that it was fortunate Willelm had been placed in a short wing of the house that had no other bedrooms. This would work in her favor, as no one else would inadvertently hear a carol meant only for his ears. She trusted that the children would be delighted to sing something special for him and would hopefully not understand too much of its hidden message.

When she opened the door, Ann and Mary cried out in delight at seeing her, and Fanny followed them over as they threw their arms about her waist.

"I have been assigned to teach you the Christmas carols that you are to sing tomorrow morning." Juliana waved the papers in front of them, her eyebrows lifted. "Are you ready to wake everyone tomorrow morning with your charming voices so that they might start their Christmas celebration properly?"

"Yes!" exclaimed both older girls. Fanny nodded solemnly.

"Very well." Juliana turned to the nurse and smiled at her. "If you go to the kitchen, I am sure Cook will be happy to give you some sugar cakes. It will give me a chance to teach the children without them being nervous before an audience."

"Yes, miss." The nurse bobbed a curtsy and went toward the door with Fanny's baby brother George in her arms, and Juliana turned to the children.

"We have three songs for you to sing in front of each door tomorrow morning. You can sing one carol in front of one door and a different one in front of the next. I wrote them down for you. Does this sound like something you can do?"

"What are the Christmas carols?" Ann asked glancing at the papers in Juliana's hand.

"'*We Wish you a Merry Christmas,' 'The First Noel,'* and *'Joy to the World.'* Do you know them all?"

Mary frowned. "I don't know all the words."

"But Miss Juliana has written them down," Ann assured her. "Do you see? We can read them as we sing, and Fanny, you can sing the parts you know!"

"Excellent. That is precisely what I was thinking." Juliana paused, reflecting on the most natural way to bring about her plan. "May I ask—who is your favorite guest here?" She bit her lip to refrain from smiling, certain of their answer.

"Mr. Armitage," Mary said, and Ann nodded. Fanny remained mute but glanced at the older girls.

"He is very good, isn't he?" Juliana said. "I know he is teaching you to ride, Ann. And he brought you a book, Mary. Fanny, do you know him?"

Fanny looked up at Juliana and nodded solemnly.

Juliana smiled. "Well. He is quite a very special friend to me, too. Don't you think he deserves his own dedicated Christmas carol?"

"Yes!" the girls exclaimed in unison. Ann clapped her hand in excitement, and Mary bounced up and down on her feet.

Now that the children were in agreement, Juliana was both relieved and nervous. She just hoped she was not making a foolish mistake. She handed Ann the three papers with the carols on them.

"Here are the carols for all the guests, and this special one is for Mr. Armitage. It is important that you remember which carol is for him. Do you see? I've put the little sketches of holiday greenery on the top of the paper here and his name on the outside. Do you think you can remember that this is only for him, and it's not for anyone else?"

The girls nodded their understanding, and Juliana added, "You can sing in front of his room last. I will teach you the special words to his carol. And then...when you are finished, you need only slip it under his door and run back to the school-room. Cook has promised to provide you with sugar cakes and all sorts of holiday treats." Juliana grinned at the children's enthusiasm, allowing it to assuage her own nervousness.

She spent one hour with the girls, which was as much as they could handle before growing distracted. At the end of it, she was fairly confident they would be able to sing her special song as well as the other ones she'd chosen.

"Remember, this is our secret," she told them before she took their leave. "We want to encourage Mr. Armitage, and we don't want anyone else to know. So when you're done singing, what must you do?"

"We fold the note and slip it under his door," Ann said.

"Precisely. You are absolute dears, and everyone will be delighted to be awakened by your singing." Juliana gave them each a kiss and made a mental note to find a small Christmas treat to give them the next day.

Despite having taken such a bold move, Juliana's heart began to beat more steadily. She had been able to transform some of those overwhelming feelings that had consumed her into action. It was a risk, but perhaps it was not too late. After all, hadn't he only just declared his feelings for her? Surely he could not so fully have transferred them to Clarissa by now.

Juliana entered the drawing room and saw that nobody was there. Then, she went to the library and looked through the window. The guests were walking in couples, although Emma had both Anthony and Matthew on either arm. Margery walked with Thomas and appeared to be saying something of a serious nature—a good cousinly scolding, from the looks of it. Farther on, she spotted Willelm walking with Clarissa, their heads bent together. Her breath caught in her throat. She hoped she had not made a mistake. It was not too late to go and tell the girls not to sing the special carol she had written for him.

But then how would she ever know if he was the right one for her? She would miss out on her chance without ever knowing what might have been. No, she needed to be bold. If she had been foolish enough to reject him in London, she now needed to be smart enough to declare that her interests had changed.

Juliana just hoped it was not too late.

# CHAPTER 16

Willelm was beginning to think that Anthony had a volatile streak. Once the man had taken it into his head that Christmas Eve in the country must comprise an outdoor excursion, he would not rest until they were all outside. Not even the ladies would be permitted to bow out. Miss Weld had seemed resigned to the idea—or to her brother's determination—and commented that the weather appeared to be mild for a Yorkshire December. Emma and Margery said they were always happy to go out of doors. And with a glance at Miss Weld, Thomas threw his support behind the idea, saying there was a charming part of the grounds they could walk to, where the heath was covered with snow.

It did suit Willelm's pleasure to be in the fresh air, but he found himself glancing often at the door to Sharow Hall, wondering when Juliana would appear.

Emma and Margery were used to the weather and were dressed warmly but not excessively. Miss Weld had covered herself very well with a fur-lined pelisse and a lined bonnet.

"If you insist upon carrying a muff, it will be hard for you to throw snowballs," Willelm teased.

"I should certainly hope throwing snow is not part of today's entertainment," Miss Weld retorted, lifting her chin in a way that might have intimidated him before he had begun to know her better.

"My sister does not know how to enjoy herself properly." Anthony picked up a mound of snow, with a wicked grin. "We shall have to pummel her with snow and see if we can get her to share our sense of fun."

"Dowsing me in ice will not cause me to become less icy," Miss Wells said drily.

Willelm thought the teasing had gone far enough, and he went up to her and bowed. "Allow me to serve as your knight errant. I will ensure that no snowballs come your way."

Her gaze held warmth and relief, and she curtsied. "You are all kindness, sir." He put out his arm, and she slipped her hand under his elbow.

They walked together, and in front of them, Emma kept turning to regale the group with what Cook was preparing for their holiday dinner. Willelm responded suitably, though his mind was elsewhere. Thomas joined them and proposed they visit the part of the grounds he had spoken of.

Margery held up her hand. "Shall I not first go and see if Juliana is done so she might come with us?"

"Allow me," Willelm replied—too eagerly, he feared—before he came to his senses and glanced at Miss Weld. "If you can do without my escort for a few minutes?"

She nodded, releasing him, but Willelm could see he had not been very gallant.

"Miss Weld, will you take my arm?" Thomas stepped forward.

She hesitated, and as Willelm walked toward the house, he heard her give an affirmative answer. Perhaps his social gaffe would be for the best. He was sure that if Thomas and Miss

Weld spent enough time together, they would reach an agreement. At least, he hoped so.

As Willelm entered the front door, he spotted Juliana coming out of the library. "Jules, we're all outdoors. Will you come?"

Juliana had been wearing a frown, and he wondered what could have troubled her. But then her brow cleared, and he almost thought he had imagined it. Her voice revealed no trace of dissatisfaction when she answered him. "I don't see how I can miss it. We have not spent enough time outdoors for my liking."

"Nor mine," Willelm said. "I will wait for you here, then."

"I shan't be but a minute." Juliana lifted the hem to her skirt and jogged lightly up the stairs. It was so different to Miss Weld's graceful movements. He loved that Juliana embraced everything with energy.

She descended the stairwell and buttoned her cloak as she reached the bottom step. "You were kind to wait. I hope the others have not suffered from your lack of escort. After all, you know the property better than any of them."

"Oh, but I wished to walk with you." Willelm gritted his teeth. That had been too obvious. "I mean to say, I intend to take full advantage of your time while you're in Yorkshire. Who knows the next time you will return? I might be walking with a cane."

Juliana laughed and bumped his shoulder as they walked outdoors. "I admit that I am enjoying my time here. I've missed the gallops across the meadows with you." They stepped into the cold air, and she lifted her face to the stark blue skies.

*She had missed him. Or at least she had missed the gallops at his side.* "But it is still your desire to return to London, is it not?" Willelm couldn't help but ask.

"I will certainly need to go back. My family is there." The snow made the sun overly bright, and Juliana squinted her eyes as she stared ahead. She hadn't exactly answered the question.

Willelm listened to the crunch of their boots as they walked along the path. The others were in the distance, and muffled sounds of their conversation carried back. Should he keep to his and Juliana's usual habit of saying whatever was on their minds? It was a risk, but he thought he saw a tiny opening, and he aimed for it.

"If we are such good friends, tell me the real reason you stayed in your room after our time together in the library. Was it truly because you had been injured?" That was direct, but Willelm's curiosity was too strong to temper his words, and he needed to know if he had made any inroads into her heart.

Juliana walked at his side in silence, her look shuttered. "If I tell you this, tell me whether Miss Weld is entertaining your suit."

Willelm's heart received a jolt of cautious optimism. Surely Juliana would not be asking that if she had no interest in him? The optimism was short-lived, though, when he reminded himself of the delicacy of his position—his own, and that of Miss Weld's, who had entrusted her secrets to him. "I have not formally proposed to Miss Weld, and therefore such a question is not one I can answer." His voice sounded formal and distant.

Juliana darted a glance at him, and he felt her tremble at his side, but perhaps that was the cold. "Oh? Why have you not? I assume she will be returning to London as well. Do you not wish to take your chances with her?"

"We have spoken some of her plans after her time in York-shire, but I am not entirely sure if she plans to return to London, or…do something else." Willelm had not expressed that with any sort of eloquence, but he could not bring himself to fabricate. Besides, he could hardly give away Miss Weld's confidence.

They had drawn nearer to the rest of the group, and Willelm looked ahead to where Miss Weld walked at Thomas's side, her arm through his. Her shoulders appeared to be stiff with emotion, and he guessed it was from unexpressed feelings. Not everyone could speak like he could with Juliana. Willelm needed to lend the two of them what assistance he could.

"She must have a tempting alternative if she is willing to consider something other than London." Juliana released his arm and hugged her own arms to her side, quickening her pace.

Willelm had always been able to read her moods, and he racked his brain to think what he had just said that would make her close up. He wanted to be conciliatory to win her back, but her words echoed in his mind. They irked him, and he couldn't help but respond to them.

"There are plenty of places that are tempting alternatives to London, you know. Yorkshire is one of them."

Juliana let out her breath in a huff. "You don't need to lecture me about Yorkshire. I am from here and am well aware of its charms. I don't need them enumerated."

"Are you?" he asked, keeping pace as she quickened her steps. "You certainly seemed to have forgotten all about its charms. They were certainly not enough of a lure to bring you back in the last three years."

Juliana's face was set in rigid lines, and she was almost at a jog now. "Well. I see Emma and Matthew ahead. Shall we hurry and join them?"

Willelm wanted to groan in frustration. "Yes, by all means. Let us do so. Heaven forbid we should be left in private, where we might say what we really think."

Juliana shot him a fulminating look and marched forward.

Later, when they all traipsed indoors, Mrs. Savile surprised the crowd with cups of hot negus that she said would be the perfect thing to remove the bite of cold. Willelm took a cup with his thanks, but left the drawing room to spend some time playing billiards alone. After he finished his drink and had spent an hour giving several satisfying cracks to the weighted balls, he was ready to think about changing for dinner. He was also ready to apologize for having allowed Juliana to feel the weight of his displeasure simply because she preferred London to Yorkshire.

He was the last to enter the drawing room before dinner. Everyone was dressed in their best clothes for the Christmas Eve festivities. Still, when he looked around the room, no one could hold a candle to Juliana, who wore a stunning shade of crimson. She was standing alone near the fireplace, and Willelm walked up to her. "You look magnificent."

She nodded, her smile frosty. "Thank you."

He did not hesitate, but touched her elbow. "I'm sorry."

She glanced at him, her look thawing slightly. "You think I have no love left for Yorkshire, but you are wrong. Having returned to it after three years has only heightened my appreciation. I may be drawn to London, but I will not forget where I come from."

Willelm wanted to respond, but Mr. Savile stood from where he had been seated next to his wife. "Friends, new and old—or shall I say, *young* and old?" He let out a laugh. "Let us begin our Christmas Eve feast."

He gestured toward the dining room with a flourish, and the guests began making their way in. Willelm had no chance to respond, so he grabbed Juliana's hand and gave it a tight squeeze as they went in. She returned it before releasing his fingers.

The Christmas Eve feast was rich, though it promised to be even more so the next day. Willelm was now full of hope and good cheer. He was making progress with Juliana, and he was enjoying the holiday in the company of others. A stark contrast to his Christmas spent alone last year.

As for the festive dinner, there was turtle soup at the bottom of the table and almond soup at the head. The goose would be reserved for the next day, along with the boar's head. But they ate venison, mincemeat pie, and three types of fowl. There were five removes, including jellies, gingerbread, and a pie at the end. Willelm partook of everything with enthusiasm and even added his mite to the general conversation, something he was usually too reserved to do.

When the meal was over, Mrs. Savile gave a look of significance to her husband. He met her gaze and stood.

"It is nearly midnight, and we have no time to waste. Follow me, if you will, into the drawing room. We must light the Yule log if we wish to keep to proper Yorkshire tradition."

The guests stood and began to file through the door into the drawing room, and Mr. Savile gestured to the footman to light the end of the stick he was holding.

"As you have probably guessed, this is the stick from last year's log." He started to bend down, then glanced at Willelm and handed him the stick instead. "My back is not what it once was. Willelm, I'll thank you to light the Yule log for me. After all, you are like one of the family."

"I am honored." Willelm took the stick in his hand and bent over to light the log that filled the massive fireplace.

He waited on one knee until it caught fire, then stood. There was a solemn moment as everyone watched the fire—as the significance of Christmas seemed to come upon them like the flickering of flames. Then Miss Weld broke the silence. She surprised Willelm by singing 'God Rest You Merry Gentlemen' with a glance at him that was very much like a wink. Before she had sung the first two lines, everyone else had joined in, and he was proud of her for breaking through her reserve.

Willelm's contented gaze traveled to Juliana. The glow of the flames lit the myriad strands in her hair and made the fabric of her dress shimmer. He glanced at her expression, of which he had a full view before she turned away, and never had he seen her more vulnerable. His breath caught in his throat. Something was shifting between them, and Juliana was not the same as when she had first arrived from London. He was nearly certain she did not view *him* the same. She was self-conscious with him now, and shyer, and it took all of Willelm's restraint not to force her feelings before she was ready to reveal them.

***

ON CHRISTMAS MORNING, Willelm woke early and threw off the bedcovers. He began to dress, although the fire had died down and the room was frigid. He barely felt it, though, from the excitement that coursed through his veins. Despite the strange tension he had had with Juliana the day before, which he had finally attributed to jealousy—at least, he hoped that was it—there had been enough clues in their interaction to allow him to hope that her feelings were changing. This hope, and the festivity of the season, left him grinning until he laughed out loud.

Perhaps it was not such a wise thing to have chosen to sleep at Sharow Hall. Without his usual tasks, he seemed to be good for nothing except to walk back and forth in his room and wonder if he had won the fair hand of one particular red-haired woman.

He pulled on his coat and, after tying on his neckcloth, went over to the window to look out at the stillness of early dawn. The sky was pink and the light still dim when he spotted the figure of Miss Weld walking outside, her shoulders slumped, in the direction of the greenhouse. There was something about her figure that looked forlorn and completely foreign to Christmas morning. It compelled Willelm to go outside after her. He grabbed his warm cloak and gloves and rushed down a back stairwell, but not before he heard the cherubic voices of the children caroling in front of the doorstep of one of the guest rooms. He would be sorry to miss such a sweet thing, but he could not let Miss Weld suffer alone.

Once outside, Willelm turned in the direction he had seen her go, and when he came to the greenhouse, it struck him as a logical place for her to have hid, so he went inside. She was sitting in the corner of the room on a barrel that had been overturned, her hands clasped together.

Willelm was afraid to frighten her, so he called out from the doorway. "Miss Weld, it is Mr. Armitage. Forgive me—I came outside when I saw you. Will you let me come speak with you?" When she didn't answer, he came forward. "Will you tell me what is the matter?"

Miss Weld had her face in her hands, and she appeared to be sobbing, although she made no noise. He pulled his handkerchief out of his coat pocket and handed it to her, and she took it and buried her face again.

"I do not wish to trespass upon your feelings," he said, his heart aching for her pain, "but perhaps I might be of assistance. You have confided in me before, and you may do so again if you wish."

Miss Weld took a few minutes to compose herself. And when she did so, she lifted her head and met Willelm's gaze, her eyes red and rimmed. "I…" She could not go on, and took a deep breath before trying again. "I turned down Mr. Sutcliffe's suit a second time last night. He does not know that I have no fortune, and I chose not to tell him. That is not what troubles me."

A deep, shuddering breath gave lie to her assurance.

"However," she continued, "after our conversation yesterday, followed by the lovely dinner the Saviles gave, it began to dawn on me that this is likely to be the last Christmas where I shall be someone's invited guest instead of attending in the guise of a paid companion. It is a very far position to fall in society, and it is difficult to bear. I merely wished to indulge in a bout of tears without letting my maid witness it. I have no doubt she is aware of what is happening in our family, but I find I need to keep my dignity in front of her."

Willelm was troubled by Miss Weld's tears, especially when he thought there was such a simple answer to her dilemma. Easier for her than for Anthony, even, because she had a solution, if only she would not be so stubborn. He had to make a push. "I am quite certain that Thomas loves you. Can you not make him aware of your circumstances—"

"I beg you will not say any more about that. I do not wish to depend on his charity. It is quite impossible for me to do, so I must put the matter out of my mind." Miss Weld's upturned face was resolute.

Willelm nodded. He needed to respect her wishes, though he didn't agree with her secrecy in this instance. He was sure Thomas was more loyal than she thought him to be. He was equally sure that Miss Weld would come to love him if only she let herself. He had promised not to betray her secret, and that frustrated him most of all because he could do nothing to help them.

He had fallen into a somewhat morose silence when it suddenly occurred to him that her brother might not be quite so fastidious. Surely Thomas's attention to his sister had not gone unnoticed. If Anthony were the one to confess their lack of fortune, then Thomas might renew his suit and be accepted, and Willelm would not have broken his word. He needed only find a way to speak to Anthony and then phrase it in a way that would make Anthony think it was his own idea.

Cheered by this plan and the near certainty that he could help her, Willelm held out his arm. "May I escort you back inside? If you are well enough, we might eat breakfast together. Otherwise, you may order chocolate in your room until you are feeling composed. After all, it is Christmas, and it is a time for cheer and good company."

"Yes, indeed. It is." Miss Weld smiled at him and stood, slipping her arm around his.

They exited the greenhouse and made their way on the path

across the snowy ground. As they walked back toward the house, Willelm saw the curtains twitch in the library, and he glanced at the window in surprise. Although the person pulled immediately out of view, he was struck by the suspicion that the face he had seen belonged to Juliana.

# CHAPTER 17

Juliana had been tossing in her bed since the middle of the
night, and she finally gave up and got up while it was still
dark. Hazel lifted her head from her cushion by the bed,
then dropped it back down as Juliana slipped into her clothes.
She dressed without help, not wishing to see anyone before she
made her way to the library. Betty would not come and assist
her for at least another two hours.

Her fingers trembled as she tied her stays, although whether
it was from the cold or anxiety over discovering her fate, she
did not know. Were she and Willelm to close the gap of friendship and discover love at last? She thought of his squeezing her
hand last night, his glances in her direction, his stepping toward
her in the library, and the kiss on her cheek. The memory made
her freeze in her movements.

As the pink light of dawn crept over her windowsill, she
cleaned her teeth, tried to yank a comb through her unruly
curls, and ended up pinning her hair back hastily. Juliana looked
in the glass and pinched her cheeks. She had gone pale with
nerves. She turned her face one way, then the other, examining
her eyes and the tone of her skin. Did he still feel the same way?

Did he long to hold her the way he had when they had ridden together after her fall?

Juliana lifted Hazel into her arms, knowing her terrier would not be happy to stay put without having had her breakfast and would likely rouse the household with her barks. Juliana then came out of the room quietly, and as she tiptoed toward the main stairwell, she heard the children singing on an adjacent corridor. There was the sound of a door opening, followed by Mrs. Taylor's exclamations of delight.

When Juliana reached the intersecting hallway, she peeked and saw that the children had moved on to the next door. She waved at them, her heartbeat quickening. They had Juliana's corridor to do next, followed by another, and then they would be at Willelm's door, where they would sing the carol written just for him. It was more like an ode, but with a Christmas sentiment. What a shock it would be when he heard the unexpected verses—words that singled him out. Would he open the door? Interrogate the children?

She pulled her wrap around her and hurried down the stairs. A maid was coming up the steps and gave a confused look at Juliana's early rising, but the maid did not halt her progress to ask if she needed anything. In the downstairs hall, noises floated up from the kitchen—preparations of holiday fare and overall festivity. It appeared the house was filled with people too excited by holiday preparations to remain abed, from the servants to the guests. At last, she sought refuge in the library and closed the door behind her.

The room was still, and she set Hazel down, where her dog began sniffing about and exploring the edges of the wall. The shelves there reached to the ceiling and were filled with leather-bound books with spines in various sizes and muted colors. A clock ticked, breaking the silence, and Juliana took a deep breath and walked over to the window. It was going to be difficult to wait.

What would Willelm do when he came in? Would he rush over and take her into his arms? For the first time in her life, Juliana longed to know what it would feel like to be kissed on her lips. She sat on the window ledge and faced the room, imagining such a kiss. The only one she could picture being that intimate with was Willelm.

She turned in her seat to look outdoors again. It had snowed overnight, covering the footprints from the day before and blanketing the ground in a soft white. Juliana pressed her fingertips against the cold glass, attempting to anchor herself to this Earth. Her heart was fluttering and flipping about in a way that was both vastly uncomfortable and wholly delightful at the same time. How was it that no one had ever told her what it felt like to be in love? Had her parents known such a sentiment? *Impossible!*

She pulled away and looked around the room, her gaze resting on the greenery she and Willelm had put up together days before. The colors had never looked more beautiful, and Christmas had never held such wonder.

True, in attaching herself to Willelm, she would be giving up London. But how could she think about accepting a cold business arrangement with somebody, having now known love? She could not. All her hopes rested on the fact that Willelm had loved her first and would surely not spurn her now, even though he had intended to pursue someone else. Oh, it was hard to wait—to know. Servants walked by the door outside in the corridor, not bothering to lower their voices. None of the guests were expected to be downstairs.

Hazel grew tired of her exploration, and she came over and nudged Juliana's leg. She picked the terrier up and held her in her arms, turning her attention back outdoors. "Hush, Hazel. Betty will bring your breakfast upstairs as she always does. It's early, you know."

Juliana noticed for the first time two sets of footprints in the snow outside the window. The sets were not lined up, and it did not seem as though the people had walked together. One set appeared to be the smaller footprint of a woman, and the other looked like that of a man. They were probably from the servants going to fetch produce in the greenhouse for the Christmas dinner.

Her breath fogged the cold glass, and she tried to calm her heartbeat as she stroked Hazel's fur. Every noise from the corridor compelled her to turn quickly in anticipation of the door opening. She could not wait to see the moment when Willelm strode into the library—the moment when he would admit he still had feelings for her. *Oh, please, Lord, let him still have feelings for me. Let it not be too late.*

A movement outdoors caught her eye, and Juliana strained to the right of the window to see. She spotted Willelm walking by first, and it took bare seconds for the implication to reach her and for her heart to shudder to a halt. If he was *outside*, then he could not have heard the carol destined specifically for him —the Christmas carol with verses asking him to meet her in the library. Before Juliana could fully assimilate that fact, she perceived in the next instant his companion.

Clarissa Weld was walking on his other side. They were leaning close to one another, her hand on his arm, and it seemed as though Clarissa's head rested on Willelm's shoulder; but then she straightened, and Juliana could not be sure.

She gasped in realization. Willelm and Clarissa were engaged! There could be no other explanation for their private *tête-à-tête* outside on Christmas morning. Juliana had been too late. She had revealed her heart to him as fully as he could have wished, but he had not been there to hear it. Instead, he had been proposing to Clarissa Weld. A silent cry rose up from within her, and when Willelm turned to look at the house, she ducked out of sight behind the curtain. Hazel whined in sympathy in Juliana's arms as her hands trembled.

Her mind worked quickly. *It's not too late to remove the evidence of my indiscretion.* How foolish had been her idea to tell Willelm how she felt about him—how forward! Juliana's breath quickened with the consequences. Willelm had not heard the carol, and if she could only remove the piece of paper from his room, then he would be none the wiser. She would not die of embarrassment.

She had to get to his room before he returned to it. Juliana hurried across the library, Hazel still panting in her arms, and she slipped out of the door. The hall was empty, so Juliana had no compunction about running upstairs. She did just that, turning around the stairwell and hurrying up the steps.

Below her, the doorway to the entryway opened, and she could hear Willelm and Clarissa's voices as they came inside. There was no time to lose. They were perhaps moments from announcing their betrothal to the other houseguests. She just had to get that paper with the lyrics. Then she would be safe.

Juliana rushed down one corridor, and then, just as she was about to turn down the hallway that led to Willelm's room, a maid crossed the path in front of her on her way to that same room. It had to be her destination—it was the only one on that end of the wing. Juliana drew back a step.

"Miss, may I help you?" The maid dropped a curtsy when she caught sight of Juliana.

Juliana kept her chin high, but she felt the heat of a deep-red blush growing up her neck and onto her face. Thank heavens she had not been found *in* his room. That would not be something she could explain away, even with him being such an old friend.

"I...I am looking for Miss Greenwood's room. Can you tell me where she has been placed?"

"Oh, miss. She's in a room on the opposite end. You've got turned about. This is the wing where the gentlemen are held."

"Oh, goodness me," Juliana replied faintly. She set Hazel

down and started to make her way back to her room, gulping down her nerves over a dry throat. She turned the corner and was nearly to her room when she heard her name called from the intersection in the corridor where she had just been.

"Jules!"

She turned slowly.

"Come," Willelm called out in an urgent whisper through his grin. He looked elated. She walked over to him, fighting to keep her dignity and her tears in check. The last thing she wanted was to hear about his engagement, but she supposed she would have to face it eventually.

When she reached him, he smiled. "Happy Christmas."

She plastered a smile on her face. "Happy Christmas to you as well."

Willelm glanced beyond her, down the hallway, then back at her. "Well, I called you over because you were the first person I thought to tell, but now I'm realizing I can't actually tell you the thing I wished because I am bound to secrecy."

Juliana assembled her face into a sympathetic expression. "That is a shame."

Willelm nodded. "I am confident that we will soon be celebrating an amazing piece of news that will be a direct result of this Christmas party. However, first it will involve a shocking piece of meddling on my part. So shocking I just know you would approve of it—if only I could talk about it." Willelm grinned and reached down to pet Hazel, who had come over to lick his boots. He stood straight, waiting for her response.

Juliana's lips lifted briefly, but she was unable to meet his gaze. "Is that all you wanted? You have news but cannot share it with me? Surely, you can share something."

Willelm's eyes lit up with delight. Mischievous delight. It was her favorite of his expressions, and the sight of it plunged her into despair. "Nay. I cannot tell you anything. Not yet."

"So you called me over only to tease me." Juliana glanced at the other end of the corridor. If only she could get to her room, where she could bury her shame in her pillow.

Willelm studied her more closely, and his look grew perplexed and concerned. "What is it, Jules? You are unwell."

Juliana shook her head. "I am very well. I am happy for your good news. I'm quite sure I shall have cause for rejoicing whenever it may be announced. Now, if you'll excuse me, I must…" Her voice trailed away, and she turned away.

She had not walked far before she paused in her steps, remembering the fatal letter that had been left in his room. She turned back around. That debacle had to be addressed.

"Well, if you should see something that surprises you, or… confuses you…I wish you will disregard it. Please know that I am absolutely delighted for…your good news—whatever it might be." It wasn't eloquent or even all that clear, but it would have to do.

He held her gaze, a look of strange confusion on his face. "Very well," he said quietly, all traces of his impish good humor gone. "I shall endeavor to disregard it, whatever it is."

# CHAPTER 18

Willelm had begun his day with what he could only describe as joyful Christmas spirit. Enchanted with the holiday spent with people he cared about, glad to have been a source of comfort to Miss Weld, delighted to have seen his way around the obstacle of having sworn himself to secrecy. He was now confident that he would have no difficulty persuading Anthony to convince Miss Weld to entertain Thomas's suit. He wasn't sure why he cared so much that Miss Weld should find a husband. It did seem an odd thing when he considered that it had not been all that long since he had thought of pursuing her himself. Perhaps it was because he was growing optimistic for his own future and wanted to spread that hope to everyone in his circle.

His enthusiasm had turned to perplexity as he spoke to Juliana, and it had quickly been followed by alarm. He had received a happy jolt at the sight of her, and he had not been able to stop himself from calling out after her. But she had been so pale and had acted as if she wished to flee from him. Meanwhile, if he'd longed to do one thing, it was to throw his arms around her and pull her close. Of course, he would not. She had made it clear how little she welcomed such an idea, and he did not want to alienate her further. He would only end up losing her friendship, as well as any hopes of love he might once have entertained.

Deep in thought, he turned his steps to his room, where the maid was just finishing her duties. His bed had been neatly arranged, the fire stoked, and his shaving items cleaned. Even his stack of letters on the desk were now in a perfect pile, with a paperweight to keep them in place. He wished she could give some lessons to the maid he employed at Lawrence House.

"I have removed the water for you, sir," the maid said, holding the basin in her arms as she neared the door. "I can bring some up fresh if you need."

Willelm went over to open the door for her so she wouldn't slop the water on her dress trying to juggle both. "No, I have no need of anything else. Merry Christmas."

She grinned at his unexpected salutation.

He pulled off his boots and laid down on the bed, his hands behind his head. What was he doing? Instead of pursuing a woman who could potentially have consented to becoming his wife, he was helping her secure a match with someone other than himself. And he was allowing his own desires for Juliana to blind him to what she really wanted: London. *Not him.* Anyone but him. He lay there for a long time, just absorbing that sober thought.

He would have to begin arranging his own future with someone else, and the thought made him sigh. He was helpless to do so while Juliana was in his sphere. He would simply need to wait until she was back in London, and he could return to his bleak existence—which was a grim thought to be entertaining on Christmas morning.

Burdened by his troubled heart and under the influence of the quiet room, Willelm dozed off. When he awoke, he pulled his boots back on and went to the breakfast room, wondering if he would see Juliana again. Everyone was there but her and Margery, who entered the room shortly after him. Christmas greetings were exchanged, and Willelm looked over at Ann and Mary Greenwood, who had been allowed to eat breakfast with the adults. Ann glanced at him with merry eyes and lifted her hand to wave. He winked at her before going to fill his plate.

The conversation flew back and forth with ease, and even Miss Weld seemed to have overcome her gloom from earlier that morning. She was making an effort to laugh and make conversation. Thomas kept his eyes on his plate or stared blankly in front of him, and although he responded whenever someone spoke to him, it was easy to see something was paining him. Mrs. Savile glanced at him more than once, her gaze sharp with speculation.

"I am surprised Juliana has not made an appearance for breakfast," she said aloud to no one in particular.

One of the maids turned from where she had been carrying in a plate of hot breads from the kitchen. "Ma'am, she charged me to tell you that she will be down in the afternoon, but that she has something to do and will take her chocolate in her room. You were not here when I came looking for you."

"Thank you, Milly," Mrs. Savile replied, glancing at her husband.

It seemed to Willelm that they spoke volumes with their eyes, and he wished for a relationship like that. He grew frustrated with himself. It seemed all he did was moon over Juliana Issot, but he already *had* a relationship like that with her. They just couldn't seem to communicate unspoken volumes about a mutual attachment.

After he had eaten, Willelm went over to Anthony, who had been speaking with Mr. Savile and was now finishing his breakfast. "Come play billiards with me. I believe we have time before the Christmas games this afternoon."

Matthew overheard the invitation from the other side of the

table. "I'll come too, so we can get up a game. Thomas, say you'll join us."

Willelm was chagrined at Matthew's proposal, for he had hoped for a chance to speak to Anthony alone about Miss Weld's situation. He wished to avoid drawing undue attention to himself by requesting a private audience.

Thomas looked up from the table, then stood. "I beg you'll excuse me. I have a mind to go for a ride."

Matthew shrugged off the billiard game easily. "Capital. Perhaps I will do that instead. It's another sunny day."

Thomas's brow lowered even further, and Emma, who had watched the exchange, called Matthew over to her. "Would you be willing to put off your ride to play backgammon with me? Margery has a project she needs to see to, and I would be glad for the company."

Willelm silently blessed Emma's insight. She would not have known that he wished to speak to Anthony, but she had seen that Thomas wanted to be alone that morning and had provided a way to entertain Matthew, who was less perceptive. He furrowed his brows as an idea occurred to him. Why should they not suit each other? He would have to ask Matthew if he had ever considered Emma Greenwood as a wife.

*Enough matchmaking*, Willelm thought, lifting his eyes heavenward. He turned back to his target. "Anthony, what do you say?"

Anthony had drunk the rest of his tea and stood. "Why not? You always give me a good game, and—"

He stopped short to listen when the sound of approaching wassailers came from outdoors. Mrs. Savile signaled to her husband. "Would you tell Gerald to come with the punch? I made sure Cook would have some ready." Her cheeks pinked with excitement, and she sent a youthful grin to Willelm. "I have missed this, you see. I cannot remember the last time I spent Christmas in Yorkshire. I wanted everything to be just so."

Willelm felt in his waistcoat pocket for the change he'd had the foresight to carry and walked to the door with the rest of the guests. The carolers piled in from the outdoors, singing "*Adestes Fideles*." He recognized some of them from the village, including the blacksmith, who removed his hat and bowed to Willelm. Their singing seemed to draw Juliana, as well, because shortly afterwards, she came into the room and stood on the edge of the crowd to listen to them.

He was glad she had not kept to her room, and he could not help but go over to her. "Now it feels like Christmas. I missed the children singing carols in front of the bedroom this morning."

"*Hmm.*" Juliana's lips were closed tight as she watched the carolers.

She still wasn't in a talkative mood, and it troubled him. How could he have so misread the state of her heart? He would have to be content to stand at her side as they listened.

When the carols were finished, the footmen brought in hot punch to warm the wassailers. Willelm stepped forward with the other guests and handed small coins to each of them. When he turned back, Juliana had left.

He swallowed his disappointment and turned back to wish the blacksmith and some of the other carolers greetings for the holidays. Anthony was near the door, and after they had seen the group off, Willelm gestured for him to follow. The two of them went to the billiard room.

As Anthony set the balls in place on the table, Willelm selected a cue. Fearing another interruption, he decided it would be wiser to get to the point without delay.

He held the cue on its end, studying the balls on the table without positioning himself. He looked at the table instead of Anthony when he spoke. "Your sister told me about your family difficulties. I promise you, I am not bringing the subject up to cause you embarrassment, and you may be assured of my discretion on the matter."

Anthony regarded him for a moment, then came over to the table. "If you're not going to shoot first, I will." He aimed for the formation of balls in the center of the table and sent the balls scattering in all directions; two of them fell in the corner and side pockets. He stood again. "I am sure the entire *ton* will be apprised of our situation before the Season begins, if they are not already."

Willelm leaned against the table as Anthony took aim a second time. One thing he had not taken into consideration in his desire to assist Miss Weld was the fact that she had not given him permission to reveal her attachment to Thomas—or that he had proposed to her twice. He would have to skirt that issue carefully.

"As I said, I would not for the life of me concern myself in your affairs...were it not for a particular issue." Willelm paused, unsure of how to proceed. It had seemed so easy when he had come up with the idea in his head. "I know Thomas Sutcliffe well, and I have strong reason to believe he formed an attachment to your sister prior to your stay here."

Anthony had taken aim, but he stood now without taking the shot. "I have noticed an interest on his side but none on my sister's. And he has not spoken a word of it to me. Surely if he were interested, he would have asked to have speech with me."

Willelm glanced out the window. He was feeling his way through this conversation and searching for wisdom in his reply. The pause was long enough that Anthony bent over and took his shot. At last, Willelm was struck with inspiration. "Thomas might not approach you without being certain that your sister returns his regard."

"He's a smart man, then. I would do no less." Anthony stood his cue on its end and met Willelm's gaze. "Please don't misunderstand me and think I wish to be rude, but are you going somewhere with this conversation?"

Willelm took a breath and plunged in. "Yes. I wanted to propose that you make Thomas aware of your family's situation. He is a man of substance, and your sister will not want for anything. And he is not the man I think he is if he rejects your sister because of your family's financial embarrassment. I have strong reason to suspect he will offer her his hand, regardless of your family's difficulties."

Anthony frowned. "I told you that my sister has not given me any clue about her own feelings. To what purpose should I take Thomas into my confidence if he will not, in the end, become a member of my family? I will have spread our family's shame to no end—and I will have taken on a gross piece of impertinence if I offer my sister to him without his invitation to do so."

*Anthony is hinting that I have taken on a gross piece of impertinence in getting involved in what was none of my affair, and he is right.*

It was Willelm's turn to take aim, and he did so now. "You said yourself that the world is likely to know of your family's situation by spring. You would not be revealing anything that will not be known, and you might do some good if she does return his regard. It might only be wanting for Thomas to tell her that he knows and that he would like to marry her despite her lack of dowry."

Anthony seemed to absorb this. He walked around the table, studying the balls but not lifting his cue. "It's a greater issue than a lack of dowry. There will be talk."

"Thomas won't care for that."

Anthony laid his cue across the rim of the table and looked directly at Willelm. "Do you know something I don't?"

"Perhaps." Willelm permitted himself a smile. "Enough to ask you to consider taking the advice—to bring Thomas into your confidence and trust that I have reason enough to recommend the course of action."

Anthony breathed out, then glanced at his ball near the corner pocket. He took aim, and it ricocheted off into the pocket. "I own that my sister—and my younger siblings—have preoccupied my mind a great deal. I have not been able to enjoy the house party as much as I had anticipated. I find that a sense of responsibility is a burdensome thing. But it would be a relief to have Clarissa settled well. Sutcliffe has his home in York, does he not?"

When Willelm nodded, Anthony looked across the room to the windows revealing the snowy grounds and chuckled softly. "You know, I cannot picture Clarissa living anywhere but London. It's almost unthinkable that she would agree."

This was an argument Willelm had long debated in his mind, and he answered from the heart. "I don't understand why this need be an issue. She can visit London any time she wants if she's so inclined. A man wants a wife, not a slave."

He took his shot, and the ball went into the pocket he had aimed for. Neither of them were focused on playing a real game. "I know Thomas will not feel any differently. Besides, if there is to be gossip, she may find it a reprieve to be in York."

Anthony laughed suddenly. "I hadn't thought of that, but I believe you may be right." He glanced at Willelm and walked around the table, holding out his hand. "Very well. I will speak to Thomas. I must thank you for your concern for my sister's welfare."

Willelm shook Anthony's hand. "Your sister deserves to be cared for. Everyone does."

# CHAPTER 19

Juliana should have remained in her room. She had been able to cry in private after Betty had brought her hot chocolate. She'd had no intention of making an appearance before the afternoon's game of charades and gift giving forced her to the drawing room. But then the sound of wassailers had approached from the road leading from the village, and she *could not* have stayed in her room while they were there.

She had only needed Willelm's reminder that he had not been in place to hear the Christmas carols to plunge her back into misery. To that cheerful observation, she had had no ready reply. Was it a veiled communication to let her know he had seen the special note the children had left for him but had kindly rejected her offer? Was he trying to be a gentleman and let her have her dignity? *Oh!* Juliana wanted to weep and stamp her feet. *The humiliation!*

The wassailers had brought their cheer and the cold in with them, and Juliana would have been thoroughly enchanted had it not been for the private distress she was enduring. Margery came up to greet her after Willelm left her side and linked her elbow through hers. They walked to a part of the drawing room away from the crowd, where it was easier to talk.

"I almost forgot to say 'Merry Christmas,' Juliana." Margery was smiling more broadly than usual.

Juliana attempted to gather her spirits enough to answer with warmth. "You are looking very cheerful today. Has the holiday brought with it pleasing reflections?"

Margery nodded, the smile fixed on her face. "Yes, to be sure. I was thinking that at this time next year, I will be married and will be celebrating Christmas in our own home in York." She looked kindly at Juliana. "You are welcome to come visit, you know. I've understood from Emma that you have a strong preference for London. However, if you should wish for a place outside of London but not quite so far north as Ripon and with more society, you need only to write. We have not met often, but I consider you something more than an acquaintance."

Juliana had a strange urge to cry again, although whether it was from the kind and unexpected invitation or from Margery's happy event that awaited her, she did not know. "That is good of you. I will keep it in mind."

When the wassailers left, Willelm was gone as well—as was Anthony. Emma was dressed with more care than usual in a sheer Indian muslin overdress to her blue satin dress. She was standing in the corner, holding her cup of punch and talking to Thomas, who had removed some of the frown from his face. Emma had a gift for soothing conversation, and Juliana had never known that before. If only she had appreciated her friendship more when she'd had the chance, they might be more than just civil acquaintances now.

When the tears threatened to rise again, Juliana grew out of all patience with herself. She decided to seek out Cook to ask when the Christmas pudding was to be served. She had expected it last night, and although she had not stirred in a wish, she had a fleeting hope that eating it might serve the purpose equally well. Perhaps she could think of her wish before the first bite.

Juliana walked through the main hall on her way to the kitchen, her holiday silk slippers muting all noise of her advancement. She was just crossing the billiard room, whose door was slightly ajar, when she heard Anthony's words as clearly as though she were in the room.

"You know, I cannot picture Clarissa living anywhere but London. It's almost unthinkable that she would agree."

Juliana stopped, her breath caught in her throat. He could only be talking to Willelm! They were discussing terms for Willelm's engagement to Clarissa; she was sure of it. Despite her abhorrence of eavesdropping, she was rooted in place and heard Willelm's answer.

"I don't understand why this need be an issue. She can visit London any time she wants if she's so inclined. A man wants a wife, not a slave."

The loud crack of the billiard shot combined with the passion in his voice sent her spinning around. As quickly as she could, Juliana made her way to the stairwell.

"Juliana."

Her godmother halted her progress, and she turned slowly.

"I am glad you didn't miss the wassailers. Milly said you had chosen to stay in your room."

Juliana forced a laugh. "I am afraid that I was so caught up in all the pleasant diversions you had planned, I have not quite finished the embroidered handkerchief I meant to have ready for you for Christmas."

Mrs. Savile raised an eyebrow and shook her head, walking over to Juliana—slowly, but without her cane. "You detest embroidery. Why do you torture yourself every year?"

Juliana's eyes widened. "Why, I thought you had a fondness for the handkerchiefs I made for you."

Her godmother rested her hand on Juliana's arm. "I treasure

them because they come from you. But I would rather you be happy. It is a gift to me when you come spend time with me and do all the things you love—ride Sunbeam, steal biscuits from Cook, play games with the children. Those are my most precious gifts from you by far."

Juliana threw her arms around her godmother, the tears welling up in her eyes at last. She would have done anything to stop them, but she was helpless against their tide. When she pulled away, her godmother examined her face with concern, her brows knit.

"Why, what is it?" she asked softly.

Juliana sniffed, and her words tumbled out. "It is nothing. You must forgive me. I am not myself. I must go to my room, but I promise to be down in time for the games this afternoon." She spun away and hurried toward the stairs, knowing she was causing her godmother to worry but unable to resist the pull of solitude.

Mrs. Savile called after her. "Whatever you like, my dear, but please do not burden yourself with making another handkerchief. I have every single one you've made for me, and they number fifteen."

As soon as Juliana reached her room, she threw herself down on her bed and sobbed. How ever would she face her all-too-perceptive godmother when she saw her later—who now knew something was amiss? She rolled to her side and looked at the flowered quilt that she had always used whenever she stayed with the Saviles, and it made her cry even harder. She loved that quilt. She loved her godmother. She loved this place.

And she would be returning to London after the Twelfth Night.

Two hours later, she thought she had herself well in hand and could face the company tolerably enough. After glancing at her complexion, which was now even again, she joined everyone in the drawing room. A footman had set up a table in the corner with a bowl of dried currants and brandy, and the children watched with wide eyes as he took a candle to set the brandy alight.

Despite herself, Juliana smiled, full of the memories. And when the children shrieked and reached little tentative hands forward before pulling them back in fright, she pulled up her sleeve and showed them how to retrieve a currant before popping the currant into her mouth.

"Jules, you're here," Willelm called out as he entered the room and walked toward the circle of chairs set up. The other guests were already seated. "We were about to play charades, and I wanted for us to wait for you."

Juliana looked at the guests gathered around him, an apologetic smile on her face that she hoped was convincing. "Please do excuse me for my tardiness. I am quite ready for our game."

She took a seat on the sofa and waited for Willelm to join them. She suffered some confusion when he sat next to her rather than his betrothed until she remembered that he had sworn himself to secrecy for the time being. Perhaps they did not wish to reveal their engagement until after the holidays. Or perhaps Anthony had sent Willelm to negotiate the settlements with their father first?

She reached out to take the paper and pencil Emma handed her and tried to compose a riddle. Normally, Juliana loved these games that showcased one's cleverness, but it was as though she had left her wits in London. The paper in front of her remained blank. Some of the other papers remained blank like hers, but a few guests were scribbling lines on theirs.

"I have one." Willelm sat up straight and glanced at her, revealing the warm eyes that always seemed to sparkle when filled with humor.

"Let's have yours, then," Margery replied. "We need not all come up with something clever before we hear the first."

"Oh, yes we do," Clarissa replied. Juliana looked down at her own blank paper. Clarissa had grown up in London. She must be filled with ideas for good riddles.

"No. You shall be bored with waiting," Matthew said, surprising everyone with his unsolicited speech. "I say we hear the charades as they come. You first, Will."

Willelm held his paper up and read from it.

*"My first is required in order to listen.*
*My second vows newness and beckons the idle.*
*But when they're combined, hope and despair are aligned,*
*for united 'tis all which is left to a person."*

THERE WAS a curious silence as the guests looked at each other. Some began to jot down notes.

"I think the first part is 'ears,'" Emma said.

"The idle person will wish to do something 'later,'" Anthony mused. "Perhaps that's it? Later?"

"Ear-later? Earlier?" Miss Weld shook her head. "It doesn't make sense. And that's not a compound word."

Despite the sorrow buried deep within her, Juliana could not help but be drawn into the game, and she remained silent, deep in thought.

At last, she gasped and looked up. "You need to *hear* in order to listen. And...and a lazy person will wish to do it later, but they might say they'll do something *after* they've finished with whatever thing they are currently enjoying. Is that it? When you combine the two, whether you're cheered or dismayed by the future, you've no choice but to accept it." She grinned and turned to Willelm next to her. "Is the word 'hereafter'?"

Willelm's smile reached his eyes. "Yes! Bravo. How quickly

you figured that out. You are clever, Juliana, and I would not expect any less from you."

His words lifted her heart as their gaze held, and his smile filled her heart with joy until reality hit and her own face fell. His smile was not for her.

She examined the paper in her hands. "I suppose we've had a lot of practice doing this."

"We have." Willelm addressed the crowd. "We used to play charades all throughout the year and not just at Christmas. This was why I wished to wait for Juliana. I could not imagine playing without her."

Juliana darted a worried look at Clarissa. A man betrothed should not admit he did not wish to play the game without another woman in attendance. Clarissa might feel crushed, although it did not seem as though her expression revealed any hurt.

"Another charade, if you please," Anthony said. "I expect to see everyone studiously bowing over their papers. You too, Matthew."

As some of the guests jotted phrases down, a footman entered the room with a note on a salver, and he handed it to Willelm. He skimmed its contents quickly and got to his feet.

"Forgive me, but I must not stay," he said with a glance at Juliana. Concerned, she kept her eyes trained on him. He could not have lost someone important to him. His family was already gone.

Willelm walked over to the Saviles and bowed before them. She was able to learn the source of his worry then, when he said, "You must excuse me from attending Christmas dinner. I've just had word that one of my ewes has died, and half the flock is sick. I will not be at ease until I see for myself what can be done."

"Of course," Mr. Savile replied, getting to his feet. "I would do the same. Let me know how we might be of assistance. Mr.

Wilkinson's man is reputed to understand sheep illnesses very well."

"Come back to us as soon as you may," Juliana's godmother added.

Willelm then turned and addressed the crowd with a bow. "I am terribly sorry. It is most unfortunate timing." He paused, his glance skittering to hers for an instant, and then he was gone. If Juliana had not thought she could feel more forlorn, she now found she was wrong.

The guests continued the game, then went to dress for dinner. Juliana visited the children in the nursery and brought them some dresses she had made for their dolls, avoiding all mention of Willelm's special carol. For dinner that evening, she leaned on her strict training in hiding all signs of distress and moved within the company as though nothing were amiss. She ate dinner with Thomas at her side, and he opened up to her more than he had in the past couple of weeks, telling her about the Thoroughbred stock he had set up and his plans to begin horse breeding with Scottish stallions.

Juliana was glad to see him acting more like himself and was heartened by the Christmas goose, the savory pudding, the molded jellies, and the long-awaited Christmas pudding. But it didn't taste as good as she had anticipated, and she didn't have the heart to make a wish.

After dinner, the guests moved to the drawing room, the men by mutual agreement having forsaken the port in favor of common entertainment.

Juliana watched as Anthony walked at Clarissa's side, providing her with what looked like comfort. If Juliana was brokenhearted that Willelm had left, Clarissa must have been even more so. Anthony had been most attentive to Emma at the dinner table, although Juliana had not noticed any deeper affection spring up between them.

After Anthony left his sister, he clapped his hand on

Thomas's back and spoke a few words to him. They left the drawing room for she knew not where. Juliana folded her arms and watched them go. Anthony was an agreeable man, and he was from London—from the very best address the Town had to offer. She imagined what it would be like to marry him while Willelm married Clarissa. They would then be joined as family. She would see Willelm at every family gathering with his children—his and *Clarissa's* children—dandled on his knee.

The taste in Juliana's mouth turned to ashes. She could *not* marry Anthony, not even with London as part of his attractions. She couldn't even be sure London was what she wanted anymore. And besides—Anthony was not Willelm.

# CHAPTER 20

Willelm threw a few essentials in his portmanteau and went out to the stable, where Mr. Savile had sent word for John Outhwaite to have his horse saddled. Dismay hastened his ride home. He should have gone earlier to check on his flock. He had allowed the pleasure of being in a family atmosphere, which he had not experienced since his mother had died, to make him conveniently forget his responsibilities. He had allowed the bliss of seeing Juliana day after day to keep him glued to her side.

When he arrived at Lawrence House, Tom Pickles was waiting for him in the stable. He came over and took the bridle to Willelm's horse before Joseph could come over. "Ah'm fain an' glad t'see yer."

"Tell me at once. How bad is it?"

Tom's expression was somber. "Layter yowe are despert ill. Eddero yowe's deed."

Good heavens. Three ewes dead, but seven more sheep ill? Willelm rubbed his face in his hands. "What are the signs of their illness?"

Tom opened his hands. "They're tetchy a' first—fagged. Then

179

they go kay-legged. Mig's akin to watter. They'll fick, sudden-like—and then they dee."

Willelm absorbed the symptoms. Irritable and tired, stiff limbs, watery stool, seizures…he truly had no idea what it could be. "Let us have a look, but I'm going to have to send word to Wilkinson, as Mr. Savile suggested." He needed someone who was more of an expert than Tom or him.

They went out to the barn where the sheep were being kept. The sight that met his eyes plunged his mood; the disease had ravaged his flock, and the ones who were ill did not look as though they would recover. The barn was unnaturally silent.

Judging from the symptoms Tom had described, it seemed that even more of his flock had fallen ill since Tom had sent word. He went over to the railing and leaned over it. One of the sheep whose limbs were stiff lay near the edge of the pen, and Willelm leaned over to see what he could make of it. There were ulcers on the side of its body.

He glanced around the barn, which was growing dark. "What did you do with the dead ones?"

"Burnt 'em."

Willelm stood upright, sighing. He didn't think he was to blame for the state of his flock, as he had done everything he could to care for them well, but he still felt the condemnation of having these animals under his care and losing them to illness. "We'll have Wilkinson's man brought in as soon as he might be available."

The next day, in response to Willelm's note, Henric Wood accompanied Willelm's servant back from Mr. Wilkinson's farm. As he, Tom, and Henric walked among the flock, they discovered that one of the rams had died as well.

Henric shook his head. "'Tis not broxy as ah'd thought," he said. "Ah've seen it afooare, and ah'm afoered tis nowt ado. We've nowt a vetnary 'n these parts."

That was the worst news. Willelm knew there was no animal

doctor nearby, so if it was beyond Henric's possibilities, there was nothing anyone could do. Willelm looked around at his sick and dying flock, the sense of helplessness settling over him like a mantle of lead. He was no expert in such matters—he never had been. But he'd had hopes of building something of his own. He had hoped to raise a thriving flock and produce something with his own hands that would bring value to the community and perhaps a legacy for his children one day. He exchanged glances with Tom. They would just have to continue to care for the sheep the best they could and bury the ones that didn't make it.

"Thank you for coming," Willelm said as he walked Henric over to his horse.

After he saw him off, he was too discouraged to return to the barn. Besides, Tom had more experience than he did and would be better equipped to care for the sheep. Instead, Willelm went to the house and greeted his head servant.

"There are letters and accounts awaiting your attention, sir," Crowther said. "Shall I have Mrs. Bell send you some dinner? It won't be what you are expecting..."

"Just tea will suit me."

Willelm sat down to his desk. He ignored the pile of accounts waiting for him and pulled out a sheet of paper to write to the Saviles. He needed to let them know the status of things and that he wouldn't be returning to Sharow Hall, at least not right away. When Crowther returned, Willelm moved his papers over so the butler could set the tea and breads down on his desk.

Willelm handed him the letter he had written. "Have this sent to Sharow Hall."

"Yes, sir." Crowther left and pulled the door shut behind him.

Willelm lit a candle, and only when he stared at his tea platter did it dawn on him that he had left the party on

Christmas Day yesterday and had missed the festive meal. He would be spending the holiday alone again.

All was silent. The house was as quiet as it always was—as quiet as it had been before he had spent those weeks at Sharow Hall. As quiet as it was likely to be for the rest of his life. He drank his tea and went over the accounts that were the most urgent. He had forgotten to bring the small stack of papers on his desk at Sharow Hall, but nothing there had been critical. Of letters, there were none of any importance and none that carried any sentimental value.

The next days passed by in a similar manner. Willelm ate alone, sat in his study, and reviewed household matters until he had caught up on everything and had nothing else to pore over. He looked over his accounts with a mind to speak to the landowner in Ripon about replacing some of his flock come August. He went out to visit his flock and watched four more sheep grow ill and three more die. Some recovered, which gave him some cause for cheer. But in truth, he found little else to give him hope.

On the last day of the year, Willelm rose from bed and considered over breakfast whether he should send his excuses to Sharow Hall for the rest of their party. He had promised he would come for the month of Christmas through Twelfth Night, but surely everyone would understand if he remained away. He stared blindly into his cup as though the tea leaves would give him the answer he needed.

He was not likely to be missed, surely. Juliana would return to London, and it would be easier not to have to see her ride off. Miss Weld had, hopefully, accepted Thomas's suit, and if she had, his help was no longer needed. If she had not, then nothing he could do would change her mind. Willelm would grow accustomed to solitude again.

He was fiddling with the handle of his teacup when

Crowther knocked and entered the room, carrying a letter. "Sir, this just came from Sharow Hall."

Willelm reached for it. "Are they waiting for an answer?"

"No, sir."

Crowther left, and Willelm turned the letter over. He saw the feminine scrawl, and his heart began to thump violently. It was Juliana's handwriting. He recognized it at a glance from years of games and riddles, although they had not written to each other before in any kind of formal way. He broke the seal and spread the paper out in front of him on the table.

DEAR WILLELM,

I HAVE LEARNED of the illness and death that has hit your flock, and I feel terribly sad for what you must endure. I know how well you care for your animals, and this loss is bound to distress you.

My godmother told me after Christmas that you had written to say you will not return at present. I understand you, but as your friend, I wished to tell you how very much you will be missed. I had hoped we might ring in the New Year together. I know I am not the only one who feels keenly the weight of your absence.

Perhaps I have no right to send you a letter at all. I am relying on our years of friendship to excuse so bold a gesture and hope you will forgive my forwardness. I will be here until the 7th of January should you wish to bid me farewell before I leave.

JULIANA

SHE HAD NOT CLOSED the letter with anything like "Affectionately" or "Yours," but it would do. She had written to him. For the first time since he'd left Sharow Hall on Christmas Day, something like a gleam of hope cut through his gloom. If Juliana had written to him, it meant she cared for him, at least as a friend. And if she cared for him as a friend, perhaps he could still get her to care for him as a woman might care for a man.

"Crowther," he called out. He would send a note to Mrs. Savile to alert her to his presence for dinner that night. And then he would leave his flock in Tom's capable hands. He had something to see to that was more important than anything else.

---

WILLELM RODE into the stable and swung down from his horse. John came forward to reach for the bridle. "Nah then." He jerked his head toward Sunbeam's stall. "Miss Issot is yonder." He led Valour to a stall on the far end, leaving Willelm alone.

Juliana came out of Sunbeam's stall. There was a stricken look in her eyes that he could not decipher, but her face was lit with a smile. She would have seen his horse pass by and known he'd come. Willelm drank in the sight of her—the sight of her smile. She dropped her face then and looked at the ground shyly.

"You're here, Jules." It was all he could think of to say.

"I could say that of you," she said, looking up. "I've always been here. You're the one who came back."

"You were not *always* here," he said quietly.

Juliana glanced back at Sunbeam, who had stuck her muzzle out of the stall. Hazel had been exploring the far end of the stable, and she ambled forward, sniffing, until she caught the scent of Willelm and gave a bark.

She trotted over, and Willelm reached down to pet her. "Well, Hazel."

He stood, and the smile returned to his face, the melancholy of the week having abated at the sight of Juliana. He folded his arms across his chest, not knowing quite what to do with them and wanting to be sure he would not use them to hug her.

Juliana shifted uncomfortably, although there was a brief glimpse of her dimples. "My godmother suggested I come out to spend time with Sunbeam since I can't ride yet. And so here I am."

Willelm could not help but wonder if Mrs. Savile had coordinated this meeting on purpose. He would thank her later if she had—and if his mission succeeded.

"It is getting close to dinner. Shall we return to the house?" He offered Juliana his arm, and she took it. As they made their way to the house, he told her about his losses. She entered so fully into his feelings, he knew she felt them as he did. Juliana had an affinity for animals, and she loved them deeply. That was one thing Yorkshire would offer her more than London. There was no shortage of animals in the north.

When they entered the house, they stood awkwardly at the bottom of the staircase before parting ways with a self-conscious smile on each of their faces. Juliana went to dress, and Willelm went to the drawing room, where he found Mr. Savile dressed for dinner and sitting comfortably on one of the chairs, reading. He looked up when Willelm came in.

"It's a sad business," Mr. Savile observed soberly. "I wish something might have been done."

Willelm nodded. "As do I."

"Well, Mrs. Savile and I are very glad you have decided to return for the New Year's Eve celebrations. After all, I fully expect you to win the vote for first-footer."

Willelm laughed. "I hardly think so, sir, but I thank you for your vote of confidence." He turned to go. "I must dress, but I shall see you shortly."

He walked into the hall and headed toward the main stairs. The front door opened, and Thomas walked in, followed by

Clarissa. She was laughing, her hand over her mouth as though she wished to stifle the evidence of her happiness. Willelm didn't want to disturb them, so he lifted his hand in greeting and turned to climb the stairs.

"Willelm." Clarissa murmured something to Thomas, who grinned at him and climbed the stairs, leaving Clarissa alone with Willelm.

He studied her for a moment. "You look happy."

She nodded, the corners of her lips upturned. "I am. It is not to be announced until Thomas can write to my father, but I think it will be hard to keep it a secret from everyone here. Still, we will not make any sort of official announcement, even among our friends here."

"I understand. I wish you very happy." Willelm held out his hand, and Clarissa put hers in it. He clasped her hand, then released it. "Shall we go upstairs? I believe we have not much time to dress before dinner."

"Oh, goodness." Miss Weld's hand flew to her mouth. "I have completely lost track of time."

She lifted her hems and jogged up the stairs, and Willelm was left to follow, happy for her...wondering if there might be happiness in store for him.

When he entered his room, he set his portmanteau down on the inside of his door and began stripping off his neckcloth. There was warm water waiting for him, and he cleaned his face and hands. He removed his riding pantaloons and pulled the silk stockings and knee breeches from his trunk. His movements were done in a hazy cloud of pleasantness—of hope. Juliana had written to him. If he could just get up his courage, he would ask her if that had meant something.

He walked by the desk, and the forgotten papers stacked on it caught his eye. For the first time, he noticed a folded sheet of paper underneath the rosewood and brass paperweight—a letter he had not seen on Christmas Day in his haste to leave for home. He went to it and lifted the paperweight. No, his eyes had not deceived him. That was Juliana's handwriting on the outside of the paper. Had she left him a second letter in his room? It did not make any sense. He opened it and began reading.

A carol? What sense was there in leaving him a letter with a common Christmas carol? Did she think he did not know the words?

*God rest you merry gentlemen*
*Let nothing you dismay*
*Remember Christ our Savior*
*Was born on Christmas Day*
*To save us all from Satan's pow'r*
*When we were gone astray*
*Oh tidings of comfort and joy*
*Comfort and joy*
*Oh tidings of comfort and joy*

HE WAS ABOUT to put the paper down when his eye caught on his name that was printed in her neat hand. What was this? He read on.

*God bless you loyal Willelm*
*Your heart ye doth display*
*Remember that our friendship*
*Was forged through childhood play*
*To bring us through the darkest hours*
*When home 'twas 'n disarray*
*Your presence is comfort and joy*
*Comfort and joy*

*Your presence is comfort and joy.*

SHE WAS RECALLING their years of friendship, which was more than he had dared to hope for. He had thought she'd forgotten everything while in London. And she wrote that he was a comfort to her. Now his eyes eagerly skimmed the next verse.

*On Yorkshire soil, near Ripon*
*My faithful friend was born*
*In London's ton, he suffered*
*From Juliana's scorn*
*Oh, foolish girl you knew not then*
*What now is plain as morn*
*Your good esteem brings comfort and joy*
*Comfort and joy*
*Your good esteem brings comfort and joy.*

HE COULD BARELY BREATHE NOW. She had admitted she had hurt him in London. She regretted it. He could scarce take in the meaning as his gaze devoured the rest of the words. What, exactly, did she mean by his "good esteem"?

*Fear not then, she did tell herself*
*Perhaps 'tis not too late*
*Perhaps she's in the library*
*To learn news of her fate*
*To free her life from misery*
*By choosing the wrong mate*

*Your love, Willelm, is comfort and joy*
*Comfort and joy*
*Your love for me brings comfort and joy.*

WILLELM'S JAW DROPPED. She wished for his love! When had she arranged to meet him in the library? Was it supposed to be for today? When had she left him this letter? He would have seen it had she slid it under his door when he was here. Besides, it had been on the stack of mail.

He gave a sharp intake of breath. On Christmas morning, when he was walking back with Clarissa, he had thought he saw her in the library. Was *that* when she left the letter? Wouldn't he have seen her slip it under the door? He began pacing back and forth. Unless she had not slipped it under his door. What if she had taught the Greenwood girls and Fanny Taylor to sing it? If she had, he had missed the most monumental thing that had ever happened to him.

Willelm glanced at the clock and saw that he had no more time to spare. But he couldn't resist raising his arm and letting out a peal of joy. She loved him! Juliana Issot loved him! And he was going to propose to that woman tonight, by George.

# CHAPTER 21

Juliana came downstairs, eager to celebrate the New Year with the other guests, particularly since Willelm had returned. The only thing that troubled her—the thing that had flown out of her mind upon seeing him, but which came rushing back when she reached her room—was that Willelm was engaged to Clarissa. Or, at least, she had been given no clue that such an engagement was not to take place. Clarissa had gone from being reserved, as she'd been at the beginning of their stay, to being downright jolly, teasing Thomas, Matthew, and her brother, each in turn. Only Willelm could have brought out that side to her. It was the behavior of a woman in love.

Juliana had trembled when she had handed the letter to the servant to bring to Willelm. It was most inappropriate for her to write to a man engaged to another woman. But Juliana had promised herself she would write to him this once, for the first and last time, if only to let him know that his friendship was important.

Christmas had been a shock. She had been sunk by the lowering discovery that it had been too late. She had loved him too late. But as the following days went by, the thought for him

—for how much he was suffering because of his troubles—became stronger than her dignity. She would write him only to bid him farewell. And she would steel her heart to meet him forever after as mere acquaintances—just as he had once warned her it would be.

Juliana understood why Willelm and Clarissa had not announced their engagement—they had had no chance to do so. But surely now that Willelm had returned, all that would change. Upon reflection, she was only surprised he had not told her of his engagement in the barn when he saw her, as true friends would have done. He had certainly looked happy enough despite his difficult week, and she—foolish woman that she was—had been lulled by his familiar smile and taken the happiness to her own credit. She had worn her heart on her sleeve. Would he and Clarissa wait until Twelfth Night to share their happy news? Perhaps they had plans to announce it tonight.

Juliana sighed and was about to ring for Betty when there was a knock on the door, and her maid came in. She went to sit in front of the glass, no longer able to produce a cheerful thought worthy of the occasion.

At dinner, Juliana was seated between Anthony and Mr. Greenwood, and Willelm was seated across from her. When she looked at him, he held her gaze and smiled, and she returned it before furrowing her brows. He did not realize he was sending her confusing messages or that he might make Clarissa jealous. But then, Clarissa was seated next to Willelm and could not see what he was doing.

The dinner began, and the conversation picked up around her, accompanied by the clink of silverware. Juliana turned to Anthony. "We are nearing the end of our stay here. Have you enjoyed Yorkshire as much as you hoped you might when accepting the invitation?"

Anthony served himself some of the pigeon. "Would you

care for some?" Juliana shook her head. He cut a piece and speared it with his fork. "In truth, I am quite pleased with how this holiday has gone. Mr. and Mrs. Savile have been all kindness. And although I did not accompany my sister in hopes that she might make an eligible match, she has done so. It's still a secret, mind you, but it will be a settled thing before long."

"Oh." Juliana's heart plunged into her toes, and her mood with it. She could not answer and tried to buy some time by sipping the wine near her plate, then coughed. "Excuse me. I have swallowed funny." She lightly tapped her chest and cleared her throat. "That is excellent news. Do you know when it will be announced?"

Anthony cut another piece of meat, then leaned in to say, "I hope by tomorrow. If not, I shall have a thing to say to both of them. Never did a courtship take so long as this one."

*So long? Theirs was a whirlwind courtship. They only met this month!* Juliana's face was set in a frown that she could not remove if she tried.

She glanced across the table at Willelm, who was still looking at her. She knew him well enough to know that he would likely have tried to force out whatever it was she was thinking if they had been sitting next to one another.

"Your attention," Mr. Savile called out from his end of the table. "I told you all at the beginning of our stay that we would be electing our first-footer for the new year, and it will be done by secret ballot. You will notice the piece of graphite and small paper placed at each person's setting. You need only note on the paper who you would like to bring good luck to this household by being the first to step through the front door. We shall trust that the person who gains that honor will indeed bring us good luck—and perhaps good news."

Juliana had not missed the graphite and paper placed in front of her, and she now pulled them closer.

"You have a few minutes to think," Mr. Savile went on.

"Then write your choice down, and we will collect the answers and announce our man over dessert."

Juliana smoothed the paper in front of her, not daring to lift her eyes from the paper. Of course, she would put Willelm. It would have to be him. He was not the tallest, nor was his hair the darkest. She was not sure how high his arches were so that "the water might flow underneath his feet." But Mr. Savile had asked for the best natured, and Willelm was surely that. In fact, he was the very best of everything. The thought made her sad because she and the very best of everything were soon to part ways.

Juliana picked up her graphite and wrote in careful letters, *Willelm*. Then she folded the paper in half and leaned back to slip it in the basket the servant held out next to her. He moved to stand behind Anthony, who put his own paper in.

Sounds of conversation and the clink of silverware resumed as Mr. Savile took the silver platter from the servant and set it in front of him without even peeking at the papers. Juliana knew he was teasing his curious guests by not revealing the elected first-footer before dessert, and she bit her lip to hide her smile. At least she could still find humor in something.

She looked across the table, and Willelm's eyes had not left her face. She held his gaze for a split second, her heart thumping, before she realized what she was doing. She was flirting. With Willelm. A man about to be engaged.

She dropped her gaze, and Mr. Savile cleared his throat. "You may bring in the sweets," he called out to the servants who were standing just outside of the dining room. He looked around at his guests as the servants set the jellies and puddings and cakes in front of them. "I suppose you will all wish to know who our first-footer is for this year. After all, we must go into the drawing room and await his entry."

"Yes, do tell us who is to bring us good luck," Mrs. Taylor said.

Mr. Savile opened the papers one by one and lay them in distinct piles, but he did not say who each one was. More teasing. One pile grew bigger than the others, and Juliana questioned whether it would be Thomas. He was generally considered the most congenial, even if he had been more broody than usual this visit. Surely it couldn't be Willelm. She was biased to think he would win.

"Our first-footer for 1816 is..." Mr. Savile glanced at his wife, his lips hovering in a smile. "Mr. Armitage."

Willelm jerked his hand, causing his spoon to clatter on his plate. "Me?"

"You are voted the most likely to bring us good luck," Mr. Savile confirmed, wearing a broad grin.

Juliana watched a variety of emotions flit across Willelm's face. He grew red and looked down, frowned, then looked up with the face of a man resigned.

"Well then. If I was voted the first-footer, I shall fulfill my role in all seriousness."

"No," Juliana said out loud, before she could stop herself. "You must do something out of character. Something...animated."

"Hear, hear," Mrs. Savile murmured as she lifted her glass, Juliana thought, to hide a smile.

Willelm sat upright and studied Juliana with narrowed eyes. "Animated! Very well," he said at last in a determined way that left her breathless. Was he going to declare his love publicly for Clarissa? Oh, she did not think she could bear it if he did.

After dinner, the men stayed behind to enjoy one glass of port while the women went to the drawing room. They were distracted with excitement for the holiday, the rich foods and elegant dresses. All of them ignored the tea that was brought in as the conversation turned to the new year. Everyone said what a relief it was that 1816 would be a fresh year without war to blight their comfort.

Juliana determined to rejoice with Clarissa rather than give in to jealousy. She walked over to her. "I believe we shall have an exciting New Year's Eve. Do you wonder what sort of unusual thing Willelm will do?"

Clarissa pursed her lips. "To own the truth, I have difficulty imagining him doing anything out of the ordinary."

"How little you know him," Juliana replied, her surprise provoking the speech before she could think the better of it. She was going to have to watch her tongue. That was not something to say to a man's betrothed, even if one did know the man better.

And...should Clarissa really be marrying Willelm if she thought he was incapable of doing something dashing?

Juliana rectified her words. "What I mean to say is, he does at times possess the element of surprise. You will see."

She was thinking of the time he climbed the side of the church just because she had said he couldn't do it. Of course, he had done the deed at night so no one would scold, but he'd left a maid's bonnet on top for her to see as proof of his daring deed. He had wrapped it around the steeple.

"*Hmm.*" Clarissa lifted her head as the men entered the drawing room, and her eyes held a soft light. Juliana thought she would be ill.

Mr. Savile pulled his wife close to him, and their dog began teasing Hazel, then scampering around to each of the guests as if sensing the excitement.

"Calm yourself, Pom," Mr. Savile scolded. "It is soon to be midnight, Willelm. I believe you know what to do. There's a bucket with some dry coal outside the door."

Willelm nodded and went out of the drawing room. Juliana heard his footsteps cross the hall, and she heard the front door open, then shut behind him. She bit her lip. He had not put on a cloak. She hoped he would not be too cold. There was a silence before the tall clock in the drawing room began to chime. Once, twice, thrice...

Juliana listened, feeling the significance of the moment. Four, five, six. Seven, eight, nine. No one moved or spoke. Ten, eleven, twelve.

At the deep chime of twelve, the front door opened, and through the silence, footsteps could be heard crossing the front hall. The door to the drawing room opened. Despite there being no reason to hope for anything good, Juliana's heart beat a steady rhythm.

Willelm walked in and set the coal on the side table and brushed his hands together. He stared solemnly at the assembly in the drawing room. The clock continued to tick the minutes of the new year, and no one moved.

At last, he spoke. "Happy New Year, to this household and to all who are visiting it."

"Happy New Year!" the voices rang out.

When Willelm stood there immobile, Juliana began to hold her breath. What was he waiting for? Mr. Savile was clearly puzzled by the pause and was as close to impatient as a man of his temperament could be.

"Come, Willelm. You must exit the back door now. You must bring the old out with you so that change and revival might come."

"And do not forget you must do something animated while you're at it," Mrs. Savile added, her expression filled with more humor and expectation than her husband's. It was as though she knew something no one else did.

Willelm turned his gaze on Juliana, and its intensity caused her blood to drain from her face. Was he experiencing regret for having proposed to another woman?

He strode over to Juliana, and, in one movement, leaned down and swept her off her feet and into his arms. Juliana's mouth dropped. The unexpected gesture was followed by a roar of laughter and animated speech.

"The door, please," he called out as he walked toward it.

Matthew leapt forward to open the drawing room door that led to the dining room and then hurried forward to open the second door that led to the end of the corridor. There was only one back door on this side of the house, and it was through the kitchen.

Willelm strode onward in that direction, his gaze fixed above Juliana's head. "Lead the way, Matthew," he said, and Matthew obeyed, jogging down the wooden steps. Willelm followed with Juliana in his iron grip. She could feel the jolt from each step.

"Willelm, what are you doing?" she asked breathlessly. He did not answer.

Matthew led them through the vast kitchen with the servants standing in two rows to usher Willelm through. They had been expecting the first-footer, but perhaps not the first-footer with a woman in his arms. Matthew opened the kitchen door and stepped aside.

"I'll take it from here," Willelm said and walked out into the snow. The kitchen door closed behind them.

Juliana felt the icy breeze immediately, and her breath clouded. She looked up at Willelm, who had his gaze fixed on her. Sudden shyness caused her to drop her gaze.

"Willelm, may I ask why you carried me out of the house?"

He smiled at her, out of breath from the exertion. "I suppose I can set you down now." He did so, then removed his coat and covered her shoulders with it.

She looked up at him, grateful for the warmth of his coat, missing his arms. "Why?"

"If you'll forgive me my presumption, I thought some of your old prejudice was better left in 1815. I took the risk that I was right and carried the old out once I'd ushered the new in. If

I am not mistaken, you have changed your perception of what you want in life. The Juliana you once were has grown a size too small and doesn't fit the Juliana of today. Tell me I am wrong."

Willelm was entirely too confident in his speech, and Juliana had difficulty adjusting to it.

"Besides, I could not very well kiss you in front of everyone."

She looked up at him in shock. "Willelm, you cannot kiss me. You are about to be engaged to Clarissa, if you are not already!"

Willelm did not respond right away, but reached into his coat pocket and pulled out a folded letter. One Juliana had no problem recognizing. She was ready for the icy ground to swallow her whole.

"Did you put this in my room?"

Juliana avoided his gaze. "No."

She felt his confusion as he looked at the letter, then at her. "Did you write these verses?"

*Drat.* "Yes."

She risked a peek at him, and he was grinning. *Insufferable.* She looked away.

"Do you still feel the same way?"

Juliana put her hands on her hips, and the gesture brought a waft of icy air onto her exposed chest. She barely felt it. "What does it matter how I feel? You are to wed Clarissa. Do you hope to retaliate for my having been uninterested in London? To crow over getting one the better of me?" Juliana hugged her arms to her chest and turned her face away. "It is better this way, anyway. I would never want to be stuck here in Yorkshire. I belong in London."

"Clarissa is to wed Thomas Sutcliffe," Willelm said dismissively, and he put both hands on her arms. "I would never crow over someone's feelings. I will make allowances for your..." He paused, and Juliana silently filled in the blank. *Hurt? Disappointment? Mortification?* "For your chagrin in having been caught out in expressing your feelings. I do know how that is. When did you leave this note? Was it for the Christmas morning caroling? Did the Greenwood girls leave it?"

Juliana nodded.

He sighed. "Jules, you must rid yourself of the idea that marriage to me means giving up London. It is true that I have no wish to remove there permanently, but I have no objection to going. And even if I am not able to stay an entire Season due to the duties that keep me on the estate, I would not hinder you from staying there if you so desired. I will just want to find suitable lodgings so that when we go—or when you go on your own —it is home."

The words rang in the air, causing Juliana to feel shame—of all the emotions she might feel, it was shame. But she thought she knew why. She had not trusted him enough to know that this was how marriage to him would be. It was an awful feeling to have been wrong and to have been so unfair. She looked up at him. "I am cold."

Willelm seemed to understand what she meant, as he always did. He pulled her to his chest, enveloping her in a warm hug.

"Heavens—your feet. I forgot." He bent over and swept her up in his arms. "You have only satin slippers on."

She looked up at him, filled with contentment and excitement. Willelm held her the way she had wished when he had carried her on his horse. He held her, not to keep her from falling, but because otherwise she was too far away.

"It is better now, anyway. I can see your face." Willelm paused, looking down at her tenderly. "Jules, I am cold, too, but I don't want to go inside until we settle this thing. I love you. I always have. I will never sacrifice your happiness for mine. Do you think you could consent to being my wife?"

She kept her gaze steady on his. "Yes, Willelm."

"Do you think if I sit on that bench on the mound of snow and freeze my…freeze my buttocks for a few minutes, you could warm my heart by letting me kiss you, as I've wanted to do these past five years at least?"

She found her mouth had suddenly gone dry, so she nodded. Willelm walked over to the bench and sat with her bundled in his arms. He pulled his arm out that had been under her legs and cupped the side of her face, brushing a curl out of the way with infinite tenderness.

He bent down and pressed his lips softly to hers, allowing his thumb to stroke her chin until her wits had fled and were wandering aimlessly around in the snow. Something awoke inside of her, and she kissed him back, bringing her hand up to pull his head closer. He responded with a strength and intent that left her breathless. They continued to kiss until he pulled back sharply, leaving her with a feeling akin to desolation.

Despite that, she grinned.

"We should...I need to..." Willelm's words trailed away. His eyes were black in the night air, and Juliana thought she might get lost in them.

"There is something to be said for snowy banks to cool one's ardor," he said at last with a dry chuckle as he pulled himself to his feet and her with him. "Are you quite certain you are ready to become Juliana Armitage?"

"Quite certain," she replied, giggling.

"Come then, love." He looked toward the kitchen door. Juliana peeked around him in time to see a cluster of faces disappear from the small kitchen window and another disappear from the study upstairs.

"Let us go announce what is to be new for 1816."

---

Sharow Estate, Sunday 7 <sup>th</sup> January, 1816

Dearest Tempie,

As you can see from the date, Twelfth Night was yesterday, and I have only just seen off the last of my guests before taking the time to write to you. In truth, I could not wait to send my letter off. I should be exhausted, but with the joy and success of my house party behind me, I can only prolong the celebration by writing about it, for it went beyond my wildest imaginings.

First, let me inform you that there was more than one match made. I hope you will not hold it against me if I am the first one to tell you that your great-niece, Clarissa Weld, has become engaged to Mr. Thomas Sutcliffe? He is my sister's grandson, and I can vouch for his impeccable lineage and his upright character. He can be somewhat of a rake at times and places a high priority on entertainment, but he will take very good care of your great-niece. Perhaps he will bring a smile to her face and lighten her rather somber expression, if you will allow me to say so. What is even more delightful, if you will consider this for a moment, is that we have now joined together our families through matrimony. I am deeply pleased that our connection now goes beyond simple friendship, although both you and I know that "mere friendship" is no paltry thing.

And now I must come to the subject at hand: my own match. You will wish to have your curiosity satisfied as to whether my Juliana has at last been won over by Willelm Armitage. She has, and it was done in a way that was most romantic. He carried her out of the house in his role as first-footer and proposed to her in the snowy garden. I hobbled over to the study at the far end of the house so I might see out the window there. There won't be any lack of passion between those two, let me tell you.

The whole thing has come about just as I hoped, with only a

trifling help on my part. Not only was Juliana won over, she has wholly embraced the idea of returning to Yorkshire to live. I suppose it helps that her future husband has promised that she shall spend as much time in London as she likes. It took until the new year for this to come about, and since I have not yet had news of you, I cannot say whether I have won our wager. Are you crowing with delight because you have at last beat me to flinders? Or are you still cleverly bringing about the match between Mr. Webb and Miss Nettles?

I never thought I would say this, but I do not mind whether you have won or I have. This Christmas celebration was so full of all that matters. We lived the month of Christmas as one hopes always to live this most special holiday—in peace and harmony; with traditions, new and old; and surrounded by our loved ones. We enjoyed the blessings of hearty fare and rich bounty in that usual way our God showers His blessings upon us—that is to say, abundantly. We had that and the promise of new matches and new life besides. Truly, what more could one wish for? I am sure you will agree that neither of us need to win a wager in order to be victorious.

I am wishing you a most truly happy, blessed Year of Our Lord, 1816. I am certain to be well enough to visit you, Margarette, Esther, and Amelie this summer when the weather is warmer and a trip to London might be thought of.

Until then, I am as always, your affectionate,
    Euota

# ACKNOWLEDGMENTS

I could not have written this book without Rod Stormes—one of my UK readers who lives in Yorkshire, who so graciously fed me information about the area of Ripon and the local culture, and who double-checked my Yorkshire dialect. He also introduced me to the special way sheep are counted and inquired whether they would get their own book. That made me chuckle. If you are curious about the disease they suffered from, they had a clostridial disease. And since antibiotics were not yet in use, there was nothing Willelm could have done to save them, unfortunately. He and Juliana would have had to rebuild their flock from the ground up the following autumn when farmers and landowners near Ripon were ready to sell sheep.

I want to give a special thanks to Gabriella Unitan, who is my cover model. We started following each other on Instagram, and I began asking her questions about how she would handle certain situations in my story so I could make Juliana more like the girl on the cover. This was the first time I've done that, and it was so much fun. I introduced a bulldog into the story because Gabbi loves pit bulls, especially the elderly ones. The bulldog in my story was a precursor to modern-day pit bulls.

I had such a blast working with the other authors in the series. It was Laura Rollins's brainchild, and she has been a dream to work with, as have Jen Geigle Johnson, Laura Beers, and Sally Britton. I hope you will get to read their books as well and see how our matchmakers fare with their mutual project.

The next in the series is Sally Britton, whose book, *A*

*Mistletoe Mismatch*, is out on Nov. 23. Click here to read Sally's book. On the next page, you'll find the rest of the books in the series.

And if you want to stay in touch, you can sign up for my newsletter on my website, jenniegoutet.com.

Have a merry Christmas!

# A CHRISTMAS MATCH BOOKS

A Wish for Father Christmas

A Sleigh Ride Kiss

A Yorkshire Carol

A Mistletoe Mismatch

A Tangled Wreath

# ABOUT THE AUTHOR

Jennie Goutet is an American-born Anglophile who lives with her French husband and their three children in a small town outside of Paris. Her imagination resides in Regency England, where her best-selling proper Regency romances are set. She is also author of the award-winning memoir *Stars Upside Down,* two contemporary romances, and a smattering of other published works. A Christian, a cook, and an inveterate klutz, Jennie writes (with increasing infrequency) about faith, food, and life—even the clumsy moments—on her blog, aladyin-france.com. If you really want to learn more about Jennie and her books, sign up for her newsletter on her author website: jenniegoutet.com.

* Photo Credit : Caroline Aoustin